I've travelled the world twice over,
Met the famous: saints and sinners,
Poets and artists, kings and queens,
Old stars and hopeful beginners,
I've been where no-one's been before,
Learned secrets from writers and cooks
All with one library ticket
To the wonderful world of books.

© JANICE JAMES.

ROSA'S DILEMMA

Solicitor Rosa Epton had vowed never to work with Malcolm Palfrey again, yet here she was, helping him defend a young couple charged with malicious damage. Working with Palfrey was no easier second time around — he became increasingly elusive as Rosa prepared the case, culminating in his non-appearance at court on the day of the trial. When Palfrey was discovered on a park bench with a bullet in his brain and a revolver beside him, was it suicide or murder?

*Books by Michael Underwood
in the Ulverscroft Large Print Series:*

CROOKED WOOD
MURDER WITH MALICE
A CLEAR CASE OF SUICIDE
DOUBLE JEOPARDY
HAND OF FATE
A PARTY TO MURDER
THE HIDDEN MAN
DEATH AT DEEPWOOD GRANGE
THE UNINVITED CORPSE
THE INJUDICIOUS JUDGE
DUAL ENIGMA
A COMPELLING CASE

MICHAEL UNDERWOOD

ROSA'S DILEMMA

Complete and Unabridged

ULVERSCROFT
Leicester

First published in Great Britain in 1990 by
Macmillan London Limited
London

First Large Print Edition
published December 1992
by arrangement with
Macmillan London Limited
London

British Library CIP Data

Underwood, Michael
Rosa's dilemma.—Large print ed.—
Ulverscroft large print series: mystery
I. Title
823.914 [F]

ISBN 0–7089–2780–7

Published by
F. A. Thorpe (Publishing) Ltd.
Anstey, Leicestershire
Set by Words & Graphics Ltd.
Anstey, Leicestershire
Printed and bound in Great Britain by
T. J. Press (Padstow) Ltd., Padstow, Cornwall

1

"MR PALFREY phoned while you were out," Stephanie said as Rosa Epton came into the office after a morning in court. "I told him I thought you'd be back around noon."

Rosa glanced at her watch and saw that it was exactly twelve o'clock. If only everyone was as coolly efficient as Stephanie, who was Snaith and Epton's telephonist cum receptionist.

"You do remember him?" she asked when Rosa didn't immediately respond.

"Once met, never forgotten," Rosa remarked. "What did he want?"

"He merely said he wished to get in touch with you as a matter of urgency."

"Well, I suppose I'd better call him back."

"I don't think he'll be there. He was leaving almost at once to drive up to town. He's going to come into the office around four o'clock. I did tell him I wasn't certain you'd be free, but he said he'd come anyway." Stephanie pulled a slight face. "He's not a very easy person to put off."

Rosa nodded her agreement with the sentiment. "I wonder what he wants . . . and what's so urgent about it?"

It was just over two years ago that Rosa and Malcolm Palfrey had found themselves co-defending in a case at Nettleford, which was where Palfrey practised as a solicitor. Palfrey and Co. was the leading firm in the district and he was its senior partner, facts he had impressed on Rosa at their first meeting. He certainly conducted himself as if the court and everyone connected with it were part of his personal fiefdom. Rosa had been relieved that the case had not required them to cross swords for, though she was the last person to run away from a fight, she wouldn't have fancied doing battle with Malcolm Palfrey on his home ground. As it was, he treated her throughout with exaggerated gallantry.

"Leave this to me, Miss Rosa," was his theme, both in and out of court.

The case in question had gone on for

about ten days and by the end Rosa felt she had enough of Mr Palfrey to last her a lifetime. But now it seemed their acquaintance was about to be renewed.

She recalled his luxurious office in a listed Georgian building in Nettleford's broad main street. It could not have been more different from Snaith and Epton's cramped premises in a drab street in London, W6.

He had also taken her to his home for lunch one day when the court rose early. It was an Elizabethan farm house (Kingsmere Farm was its name) about four miles from Nettleford, with an interior that had been expensively, but tastefully, modernised. Rosa's impression of Mrs Palfrey had been of a quiet but alert woman. Her name was Nadine and Rosa gathered she was Italian by birth but with a fair amount of Slav blood in her veins. She came from that part of Italy that adjoined Yugoslavia and which had changed hands over the centuries. There had also been two exceptionally well-behaved children, Teresa twelve and Cressida ten, who, at their father's direction, had greeted Rosa with demure curtsies. It had not surprised her to discover that his writ ran as strongly in his home as elsewhere. Nevertheless, it had also been apparent that he had genuine affection for his wife and children.

On the drive back to court after lunch he had confided that he still very much hoped to have a son. He told Rosa that he was forty-six and his wife forty and that he realised time was running out as far as she was concerned. He made it plain that his own virility was not in question.

"The thing is, Miss Rosa," he had gone on, "I'm the heir to an old family baronetcy and I'm naturally anxious to have a son to whom the title can be passed on in the fullness of time. Our whole social structure rests on continuity and should I die without an heir, that would be an end to the baronetry. After over a hundred years!"

The present holder of the title, he told Rosa, was a second cousin, Sir Clement Palfrey, who was unmarried and had no brothers or closer relative than himself. Moreover, Sir Clement was now in his eighties.

"He could die any day," Malcolm Palfrey remarked with the air of a judge passing sentence.

As she listened to him, Rosa had reflected on people's differing priorities. A title was the last thing she aspired to. She had once been briefly courted by the son of an earl, but the prospect of one day becoming a countess mattered to her far less than the fact he suffered from bad breath. Nevertheless, she hoped for the sake of joy and harmony in the Palfrey home that his wish to father a son might be fulfilled.

It had been about fifteen months later she had spotted a notice in the births' column of *The Times*. It read:

Palfrey, to Nadine and Malcolm, a son, Crispin, a brother for Teresa and Cressida.

She had pictured Teresa and Cressida bent solemnly over a cot. Baby Crispin was unlikely to lack attention. She wondered whether she should congratulate Malcolm Palfrey on the happy event when he arrived, or leave him to mention

5

it; something she felt sure he would do at the first opportunity.

It was a few minutes after three-thirty when Stephanie, in her most expressionless voice, announced that Mr Palfrey had arrived and was in reception, the somewhat grand name for the draughty entrance lobby. Rosa couldn't help wondering if he had arrived deliberately early to forestall her slipping out of the office to avoid him. She realised at once, however, it was a foolish notion as Malcolm Palfrey would never envisage anyone wishing to avoid him.

As she walked along the corridor to welcome him, she could see him sitting on the edge of his chair, glancing around with an air of undisguised disdain. Snaith and Epton had never believed in spending money on fripperies merely to impress their clients, most of whom would infer from any display of opulence that the firm was into high profits, which was certainly not the case.

"Hello, Miss Rosa," he said, jumping up and coming forward with outstretched hand. "It's good to see you again. Sorry to burst in at such short notice, but as your girl probably told you, I come on a matter of some urgency."

"Come along to my room and tell me what I can do to help," Rosa said.

Although he didn't appear to have changed, Rosa sensed that he wasn't entirely at ease. She presumed the reason might shortly emerge.

He had an elegant black document case which he now unzipped, removing a single sheet of paper which he studied for a moment with a thoughtful expression.

"I'm hoping, Miss Rosa," he said, still staring at the piece of paper in his hand, "that you'll agree to co-defend with me again." Looking up and giving her a confident smile, he went on, "I thought we got on pretty well together last time and I couldn't think of anyone better to approach in the present slightly difficult circumstances." He let out a sigh and stroked his chin with judicial gravity. "It's the old, familiar story, Miss Rosa, one agrees to defend two people who are jointly charged, not anticipating any problems and subsequently a conflict of interest arises which requires them to be separately represented. I want you to undertake the defence of one of them. His name is Jeremy Scott-Pearce. His co-defendant is a girl named Amanda Ritchie, whom I shall continue to represent." Then, as though dangling a particularly succulent piece of bait under her nose, he added, "I should mention that both come from well-to-do families who can afford to pay for their defences, so there's no question of a pittance from the legal aid fund. The case has, at least, that attraction."

"What are they charged with?" Rosa asked in a brisk tone, not wanting to give her visitor the impression that a handsome fee was all that mattered, though it was certainly a powerful incentive.

"Good question, Miss Rosa. They're jointly charged with causing malicious damage and with a number of minor motoring offences, all the result of a single escapade one evening in late October. As a matter of fact it was three weeks ago this very day."

"How old are they?"

"Jeremy's twenty-one and Amanda is about eighteen months older. They both grew up locally, though their families have now left the district. Jeremy's parents split up about five years ago when his father went off with a younger woman. His father now lives in Geneva and his ex-wife moved to London. Jeremy lives with his mother, but visits friends in the Nettleford area from time to time." He pursed his lips. "Amanda is the daughter of Arthur Ritchie, who was my partner until he had a coronary and decided to bow out of the law. Arthur and his wife now live in Gloucestershire. Amanda's a sweet girl, though she's always been a bit headstrong. Incidentally, she's my godchild. That's why I feel, when it comes to a choice, I must continue to look after her interests."

Rosa wondered if that were the only reason.

"What exactly did they do?" she asked when Mr Palfrey seemed to go into a reverie. There had certainly been none of those the last time they met.

"There was a party on the evening in question in the village hall at Little Nettleford. That's about three miles from Nettleford itself. Jeremy and Amanda were among the invited guests, who numbered about sixty. There was obviously too much drink about and not enough supervision. The people who gave it have more money than sense and have always indulged their daughter whose birthday it was. It went on into the small hours. Amanda and Jeremy left together in his car and, as far as everyone else was concerned, disappeared into the night." He let out a sigh. "More's the pity they didn't do just that! However, they were obviously drink-taken and decided the night was still ripe for some fun." He gave another sigh. "One of my neighbours is a certain Oliver Anstey. He's a wealthy man and a thoroughly obnoxious one, to boot. He's always complaining about something or other and demanding what he calls 'appropriate action'. He and I crossed swords some while ago when I declined to act for him in one of his many disputes with the local authority. He was furious and has never forgiven me, not that that causes me to lose any sleep." There came a third sigh. "Nevertheless it was extremely unwise of Amanda and Jeremy to select him as the victim of their prank. It was like prodding a poisonous snake for a bit of fun."

"What exactly did they do?"

"They put a firework though his letter box. An ignited firework. It went off with a loud bang, scared everyone in the house and burnt a hole in a valuable Chinese rug."

"I suppose it might have burnt the house down," Rosa remarked.

"But it didn't and I think we can accept it was never their intention to endanger life. Indeed, the crown hasn't charged them under the sub-section of the Criminal Damage Act that incorporates an intention to endanger life."

"What are they charged with then? Sub-sections One and Three of Section One?"

"Spot on, Miss Rosa; both of which, as you will know, can be dealt with summarily. The trouble is that Oliver Anstey is determined to turn the whole affair into a state trial. He's bringing all the pressure to bear that he can to ensure the case goes to the crown court."

"From what you've said, I gather he's not without a certain amount of clout."

"But then neither am I, Miss Rosa."
With a judicial air he went on, "It was
a stupid, even dangerous, thing to do,
but it hardly amounts to high treason.
Anstey's aware of his reputation as an
awkward cuss and there's not much
doubt that his dignity suffered as much
as his precious rug."

"I take it they're both on bail?"

"Yes. I had no problem persuading
the court to grant them bail. A condition
was that they should stay away from
one another, but that didn't present
any difficulty. Amanda is with friends
in Kent and Jeremy's at his mother's
flat in town."

Rosa waited while her visitor seemed
to become lost in thought. She had the
impression that he had more on his
mind than the fate of Jeremy Scott-
Pearce and Amanda Ritchie. As the
silence continued she glanced quickly
at her watch which seemed to produce
the desired effect.

"And now this conflict of interest
has arisen and I'd like you to help
me," he said, mentally shaking himself.
"Originally they seemed prepared to

share the blame for what happened, but Amanda is now saying that it was entirely Jeremy's idea to put the firework through Anstey's letter box and that she was too drunk to know what was happening."

"But Jeremy doesn't accept that?"

Mr Palfrey shook his head. "He still maintains that it was a joint enterprise."

"So it looks like turning into a cut-throat defence?"

"I'm sure that can be avoided. If the magistrates agree to deal with the case and they both plead guilty, the whole matter can be dealt with by way of a fine or something of that order. I think you can safely leave that side of it to me, Miss Rosa. I know all the justices who sit on the Nettleford bench and I have the clerk of the court in my pocket."

"What about the prosecutor?"

Mr Palfrey gave a contemptuous snort. "An apparatchik," he said.

"Have you told Jeremy that you think he should be separately represented?"

He gave a slow nod.

"And?"

"And nothing, Miss Rosa."

"I meant, what was his reaction?"

13

"I presented him with a *fait accompli*."

"Was he aware that Amanda was throwing all the blame on him?"

"I explained the position fully to him," Mr Palfrey said with hauteur, then quickly went on, "With your permission, I shall give him your name and telephone number and leave you to get in touch with one another. Charles Scott-Pearce, his father, is a very wealthy man and money will be no object where his son's defence is concerned. There's always been a strong bond between him and Jeremy and I suspect he feels guilty about the divorce. Jeremy was fifteen at the time and didn't take his parents' break-up at all well." He pulled a document from his briefcase. "Here's the statement I took from Jeremy. I'll leave it with you and give you a call tomorrow, Miss Rosa, when I hope to receive your agreement to represent him. You'll be doing me a great favour and taking a weight off my mind." He gave her a resigned smile. "He's a nice lad and deserves the best. That's why you immediately came to mind when I decided I couldn't represent them both." He rose to his feet, "Well, I mustn't take

14

up more of your time. Also I'd like to be on my way before the evening rush hour reaches a peak."

"I used to reckon to drive to Nettleford in just under an hour," Rosa remarked.

"Sometimes more, sometimes less depending on the time of day."

"Do you still have your Mercedes?"

"Not the same one," he said in a tone of mild reproof. "It pays to have a new one every year. I seem to remember you drove a small Honda."

"I still do. The same one," Rosa said with a smile.

They moved towards the door. To Rosa's surprise, he still hadn't mentioned the birth of his son and she wondered if there had been some subsequent tragedy she knew nothing about — that the baby had died or been born deformed, perhaps.

"How are your family?" she enquired as they reached the corridor.

"They're all well, thank you, Miss Rosa. Cressida's just gone to a new school and has settled down very quickly. She makes friends more easily than Teresa." He hesitated a moment before going on.

"There's been an addition to the family since I saw you last. Young Crispin was born on the tenth of July last year.

"Congratulations. I remember that you were hoping to have a son."

He nodded. "Yes, indeed."

"And your wife's well?"

"Yes. We have a very good Italian girl living in. She's not a trained nanny — Nadine didn't want that — but Italians have always had a wonderful way with children. Apt to spoil them and smother them with affection, but that doesn't matter at Crispin's age."

"So one day there'll be a Sir Crispin Palfrey," Rosa remarked in a tone that carried the merest trace of mockery. She was sure Mr Palfrey wouldn't notice it and he certainly didn't appear to do so.

"My old cousin's still alive, defying his doctors and the Almighty, but he can't last much longer."

"Nevertheless, I expect you're pleased that the line of succession has been secured."

"Of course. It's lifted a great weight off my mind. Not to mention brought joy to my wife and myself."

They reached the main door and he turned. "It's been good seeing you again, Miss Rosa, and I hope I can rely on your help. Once you say the word, we can discuss tactics."

"When are they due to appear in court?"

"Thursday the week after next. I'd like to have everything sewn up by then."

Rosa was still in reception talking to Stephanie when Robin Snaith came in.

"Was that a client I just met leaving the building?" he enquired.

"*That*," Rosa replied, "was Malcolm Palfrey, solicitor of Nettleford."

"Ah! That also explains the Mercedes parked on a double yellow line."

Rosa followed her partner to his room to tell him about Mr Palfrey's visit.

"Why didn't you agree to his proposal straight away?" Robin asked when she had finished.

"Because I didn't want him to think he could buy me. He rather over-played the fact that it was a privately paid defence, as though I'd fall at his feet in gratitude."

Robin laughed. "Pure, incorruptible Rosa!" Then in a change of tone he went on, "But you will phone him tomorrow and say yes. Yes?"

"Of course; I'm not *that* incorruptible."

2

WHEN Rosa phoned Malcolm Palfrey's office the next morning, she was told he was out, but that she could be put through to his secretary. She wondered if it was the same one she had encountered previously, a redoubtable middle-aged woman whose name she didn't remember. Mr Palfrey always referred to her as his faithful Brünnhilde as she had the proportions of an old-style Wagnerian soprano.

"Mr Palfrey's secretary speaking," a voice said at the other end of the line. "Is that Miss Epton?"

"Yes, I promised to call Mr Palfrey this morning — "

"Yes, he told me, Miss Epton, and asked that you leave a message.

"Will you tell him that I agree to represent Mr Scott-Pearce?"

"Of course. I know he'll be pleased, though I think he was expecting that answer. I'll let him know as soon as he comes in."

Rosa was almost sure it was the same woman as before and felt that courtesy required her to refer to their having met.

"I believe we met when I did a case in Nettleford a couple of years ago."

"That's right, I've been Mr Palfrey's secretary for over ten years," she gushed.

"That's a proud record."

"It's kind of you to say so, Miss Epton."

In the usual way of things, Rosa recalled her name just as she rang off It was Seeberg, Madge Seeberg. Though Mr Palfrey was the only person in the office permitted to address her by her first name.

Having communicated her decision, Rosa could see no reason not to get in touch with Jeremy Scott-Pearce immediately. The sooner she met him the better, and as he lived in London she didn't anticipate any problem.

A woman answered the phone and said he was in the shower, having only just got up.

"Do you want me to tell him you called?" the voice enquired, obviously hoping the answer would be no.

"It's all right, I'll ring again in about ten minutes."

The puritan streak in Rosa was affronted that a twenty-one-year-old was only just out of bed at eleven o'clock in the morning.

When she phoned back, a male voice answered.

"Is that Mr Scott-Pearce? Mr Jeremy Scott-Pearce?" she asked in a none too friendly voice.

"Yes."

"My name's Rosa Epton."

"Who?"

"Rosa Epton."

"I remember. We met at Jenny's party the other evening."

"I wasn't at Jenny's party," Rosa said, this time trying not to sound too stuffy. "I'm a solicitor. I had a visit yesterday from Malcolm Palfrey."

"Oh you're the person who's going to defend me now that he's ducking out."

Despite the words, he spoke without apparent rancour.

"I think it would be a good idea if we met soon and discussed the case."

"Sure, when do you suggest?"

"I'm free this afternoon.

"What time?"

"Three-thirty."

"Where do you hang out?"

Rosa gave him the address.

"OK, I'll see you around three-thirty."

"Not around, at."

He laughed good-humouredly. "I'll be there. As a matter of fact, I'll be interested to hear what Malcolm's told you."

From the voice on the phone, Rosa had the picture of a breezy young man who wasn't exactly worn down by a sense of responsibility. That was borne out by what he and Amanda were alleged to have done. She imagined he would probably regard jeans and a T-shirt as appropriate dress for visiting a solicitor in W6, which was not one of London's more fashionable areas. Especially as he was coming from his mother's flat in Chelsea's Tite Street.

She was therefore considerably surprised when a well-groomed young man in a dark suit arrived on the dot of three-thirty. Spectacles gave him a mildly studious air and his haircut might have received a sergeant major's seal of approval. In fact, he looked the last sort of person to push lighted fireworks through people's letter boxes. But then Rosa had seen enough of human nature to know that physical appearances could be totally misleading.

"A bit different from Malcolm's office," he said with a disarming grin as he looked about him. Then quickly he added, "I'm sorry, that sounded rude, but it wasn't meant to be."

"Just a verbal firework through my letter box?" Rosa remarked.

"OK, so where do we start?"

"With the statement you gave Mr Palfrey. I note you say that it was a joint idea to go to Mr Anstey's house when you and Amanda left the party. But one of you must have been first to come up with it. Was it you or Amanda?"

"I honestly don't remember. We really did seem to think of it together."

"At what stage of the evening was that?"

"When we went outside to watch the firework display. I had one of those cracker things that jump about and throw off coloured sparks and more or less at the same moment we said, 'Let's', to each other. We had been talking about old Anstey just before, saying it was time he got some form of come-uppance."

"So did you drive straight to his house?"

"We stopped on the way and had a bit of a smooch."

"That's not in your statement."

He shrugged. "I'm sure I mentioned it to Malcolm. Perhaps he didn't consider it relevant."

"Probably not. Is — or should I say, was — Amanda your steady girlfriend?"

"Good Lord, no. We just happen to have known each other since we were kids." He gave his head a bewildered shake. "I just don't understand what she's up to."

"I was going to ask you about that," Rosa said. "Why do you think she's suddenly putting all the blame on to you?"

"It must be her father. He's been

crankier than ever since his heart attack and he's pushed her into saying it was all my doing. I need to have a talk with her, but I don't know where she's staying, except that it's somewhere in Kent."

"I believe it was a condition of bail that you shouldn't see each other."

"A friend of mine who's studying law says it's an unenforceable condition, so they can sod off."

"I don't advise your putting it to the test," Rosa said firmly.

"I can't, anyway, if I don't know where she is."

The corners of his mouth had gone down giving him the air of a recalcitrant schoolboy.

"I suppose somebody spotted you driving away from the Anstey's house?"

He nodded. "I've got a red MG and it's pretty well known round Nettleford. Too well known. Even if people can't identify its colour after dark, its noise is unmistakable."

"So Mr Anstey would have known as soon as you drove away?"

"Yes."

"When did the police actually get on to you?"

"Amanda and I were both staying with some people called Seymour who live in the district. Their son, Harry, was at the party and about half a dozen of us dossed down at the Seymours. The police had no difficulty finding out where we were."

"I suppose you could perfectly well have driven back to London?" Rosa said thoughtfully.

"Sure."

"What I'm getting at is that you didn't immediately put as much distance as possible between yourself and Nettleford."

"Correct. Why should we have? It was only intended as a practical joke."

"A somewhat dangerous one," Rosa remarked in a disapproving tone. She had always had an aversion to practical jokes, regarding them as singularly one-sided forms of amusement with the selected victim being given no say in his fate.

"The firework was a bit livelier than we'd expected," he said with a shrug.

"You're lucky it woke up the family or you could have found yourself facing an even more serious charge. Supposing the house had caught fire and there'd been a loss of life?"

He frowned. "But it didn't and there wasn't. I'd prefer it if you didn't lecture me. I had enough of that from Malcolm. As if he had a monopoly on virtue," he added scornfully.

"I expect he feels entitled to as he's known you all your life."

"Sometimes it seems longer than that! Malcolm should have been born a century earlier, he'd have made a good Victorian paterfamilias."

"Do you know his wife?" Rosa enquired curiously.

"Nadine's a lovely person. She's always been sweet to me. I reckon she has a lot to put up with."

It was apparent that Jeremy had no fond feelings for Malcolm Palfrey and that this wasn't purely the result of the solicitor having thrown him over.

He now went on, "You're probably wondering why I asked him to defend me in the first place seeing that he's not my favourite person. The answer is that he's Amanda's family solicitor and we went along to see him together. It was the obvious thing to do in the circumstances. I couldn't foresee what was going to happen, could I?"

"But now you're annoyed with him," Rosa observed, as though thinking aloud.

"Puzzled more than annoyed. I just don't understand what Amanda's up to. I'd hoped Malcolm might have filled you in on the background. Did he?"

Rosa shook her head. "Merely that a conflict of interest having arisen, he realised he could no longer represent you both."

"So you get lumbered with me instead."

"You don't have to accept my services any more than I'm obliged to act for you," Rosa remarked crisply.

"Are you saying you'd like to be shot of me too?"

"No; merely that you don't have to engage me as your solicitor simply because Malcolm Palfrey has proposed the arrangement. Maybe you'd like to think it over and discuss the position with your mother or father?"

"I phoned my father in Geneva last night. Malcolm had already spoken to him. Apparently he'd given you his gold seal of approval and Dad told me to behave myself when I met you." He gave Rosa a quizzical look. "Dad wondered if Malcolm hadn't engineered the whole thing."

"You mean, he'd put Amanda up to throwing all the blame on to you?"

"Yes."

"But why?"

Jeremy gave her a blank look and shrugged. He was clearly not prepared to speculate further and Rosa had the impression he had suffered a sudden change of mind.

After a silence she said, "Mr Palfrey seems confident he can persuade the magistrates' court to deal with the case, in which event my advice would be to plead guilty and leave me to mitigate. It's one of those offences with varying degrees of seriousness and I hope a court would take the view that what you did was at the lower end of the scale."

"That's all very well, but supposing Malcolm stands up and says it was all my fault and there's Amanda looking pure and virginal, the court's not going to look on me very kindly in those circumstances."

"I'll obviously have to find out exactly what Mr Palfrey will say about his client's responsibility. You can leave me to discuss all those aspects with him before we get to court.

"And what about this bloody man Anstey who'd like to see us both taken off to the Tower of London and beheaded?"

"Unless he can pull strings with the Crown Prosecution Service, he can't influence events in court. Being the injured party doesn't give him a say as to how the case should be tried." She glanced down at the pad on which she had been making notes. "I'll be in touch with you again before we go to court. I'll also make contact with the police and have further discussion with Mr Palfrey." She paused and frowned. "I've not asked you yet, but what exactly do you do? I see your statement describes you as a student. A student of what?"

"You could say, of life," he said with a faint smile. "Actually, my father's trying to get me into a business school in Lausanne and the idea is that I go there in January. Thereafter, who knows? I can think of masses of things I don't want to do, but nothing that holds out any appeal for me. I know I'd hate to work in an office, but I'd equally detest being a forest ranger. As for accountancy or the law, no thank you."

"An astronaut perhaps," Rosa remarked sardonically.

He gave her a small, sour smile. "I'd sooner go to prison than into space." With a sigh he went on, "My father's mad about young people gaining experience. Well, at least I'm doing that." He got up to leave. "Incidentally, you may get a call from my father. I know Malcolm gave him your number. If he does ring, tell him not to worry about me."

Rosa didn't necessarily believe that first impressions were right. Moreover, she found it hard to sum up her impression of Jeremy Scott-Pearce. Fortunately she wasn't required to like her clients; not that she had positively disliked him. He was obviously a feckless young man, probably spoilt and selfish into the bargain, but not without an attractive seam in his make-up.

31

It was about thirty minutes after his departure that her phone gave a peremptory buzz.

"I have a Mr Scott-Pearce on the line," Stephanie announced, adding, "Father of the one who's just left."

"Oh! You'd better put him through."

"Miss Epton? I'm Charles Scott-Pearce," a brisk voice said a moment later. "I understand that Malcolm Palfrey's spoken to you about defending my son."

"Also your son's been to see me this afternoon."

"Ah! So you know all about everything."

"I know what Mr Palfrey and your son have each told me," Rosa replied cautiously.

"Palfrey says you're a very capable lawyer, Miss Epton, so I hope you'll be able to get Jeremy off."

"I don't think that's a viable option. I've already told him he'll have to plead guilty. There can't be any dispute about the facts."

"But it was no more than a silly prank. He and Amanda had probably had a bit too much to drink and I

32

assure you that nobody who knows Oliver Anstey is going to feel any sympathy for him."

"You may call it a prank, but in the eyes of the law it was a criminal offence. A serious one at that."

"I'm quite sure they never intended any harm."

"People are presumed to intend the natural and probable consequences of their acts and the natural and probable consequence of pushing a lighted firework through someone's letter box is to cause damage. I can't help thinking they're fortunate not to have been charged with the offence that alleges an intent to endanger life. Let's hope that still doesn't happen."

"You mean it could?"

"Certainly. The prosecution could easily decide to add a further charge."

"Supposing that doesn't happen and Jeremy pleads guilty as you propose, what can he expect to get?"

"If we can have the matter dealt with summarily by the magistrates, it would be my guess that he'll be fined."

"I see," he said thoughtfully. "It's

important not to let Palfrey get away with putting all the blame on to my son." After a pause he added, "I don't know what he's up to."

"I imagine Amanda has been under pressure to change her story. Jeremy suggested it was her parents."

"I wonder. I just wonder." He was silent for a while before continuing. "I'm not at all happy with what Palfrey's done — no disrespect to you, Miss Epton — and I told him so when he called me. I wish I'd been able to fly over immediately, but it wasn't possible, but I'll certainly come next week. I'm very close to my son and I want him to feel fully supported." In an aggressive tone he added, "Malcolm Palfrey and Oliver Anstey aren't the only people with influence in the district."

"Look, Mr Scott-Pearce, if you wish to make other arrangements for your son's defence, you're at perfect liberty to do so."

"I don't wish to, but that still doesn't prevent me feeling annoyed at what's happened. Don't get me wrong, Miss Epton, none of this is meant as a reflection on you. From all I hear, Jeremy couldn't be in better hands. And Malcolm Palfrey isn't my only source of information as to that." Leaving Rosa to wonder who else he had spoken to about her abilities, he went on, "Palfrey and Co. is still a good firm despite its warring partners. Of course, George Ritchie has now retired following his heart attack, but Adrian Chance is still there. You've met him, I suppose?"

"No."

"He's the second partner, though he and Palfrey are scarcely on speaking terms. All to do with the carve-up that took place when Ritchie left. Chance felt he'd been cheated."

Rosa had no great wish to be told about the divisions in Malcolm Palfrey's firm. They certainly had no bearing on Jeremy Scott-Pearce's defence to a charge of criminal damage.

"I'd better give you my phone number so that you can call me at my office in Geneva," Charles Scott-Pearce went on. "I'll also put a cheque in the post to you. Will two and a half thousand suffice as an opening payment?"

Rosa didn't like to enquire whether he was referring to pounds sterling or Swiss francs. In any event, the amount was acceptable in either currency.

"There is one point I should ask you about," she said before he rang off "Do you know if Jeremy's mother is likely to get in touch with me?"

"I most certainly hope not," he said vigorously. "Jeremy is little more than a lodger in his mother's flat and I'd be much happier if he didn't live under her influence. She's an adept mischief-maker. And I can think of no reason for you to get in touch with her. If she happens to answer the phone when you're calling Jeremy, I suggest you decline to be drawn into any discussion of the case."

"I'll bear in mind what you've said," Rosa observed in a neutral voice.

It was clear that Charles Scott-Pearce had no love for his ex-wife. It was possible the sentiment was reciprocated. After all, it had been he who had left her for a younger woman. Rosa certainly had no wish to become involved in their continuing marital warfare.

She became aware that he had something further he wished to say and waited for him to speak.

"Did Palfrey mention Jeremy's previous spot of bother?" he asked in a hesitant tone.

"No. But I'd better know about it."

"I'm surprised he didn't tell you," he said sardonically. "Jeremy had to leave school early. By which I mean he was expelled."

"A lot of boys are, without its necessarily clouding their adult lives."

She supposed he had been caught in bed with a younger boy or something of that sort. She was certainly unprepared for what followed.

"He was expelled for blackmail."

"Oh! Whom did he blackmail?"

"One of the masters whom he found lying in the bushes with a young Portuguese, who worked in the school kitchen. He'd come over as a foreign student and was only nineteen. Eventually the master could stand it no longer and killed himself, leaving a note saying why he'd decided to take his life."

"I take it the police were involved

as there would have to have been an inquest?"

"Yes, but everything was hushed up as far as possible. The Portuguese youth returned to his own country and Jeremy was expelled."

"How old was he at the time?"

"Sixteen. My wife and I had just broken up and it was accepted that Jeremy had been severely traumatised by the divorce."

"How much money did he extract from the master?"

"Several hundred pounds in weekly payments of fifty pounds."

Rosa blinked as she stared at the chair in which Jeremy Scott-Pearce had recently been sitting.

3

"HURRY up, darling, or you'll keep everyone waiting," Nadine Palfrey called upstairs to Teresa. She had spotted the school mini-bus that collected the girls turning into the drive. Cressida, her younger daughter, was already standing by the front door.

With both girls now going to the same school, life should have been easier, but Teresa was going through a rebellious period which manifested itself in untidiness and a disregard for punctuality. Fortunately, Cressida showed no sign of following her sister's example.

Teresa now appeared at the top of the stairs and descended with the air of a leading lady making her grand entrance. Her mother held the front door open and Teresa sailed past, pausing only to accept a quick kiss on the cheek.

Apart from Maria who was giving Crispin his morning bath, Nadine had the house to herself Malcolm having already left for his office.

Mrs Drake, her cleaning woman, would arrive shortly on her motor scooter to start her round of daily chores. This meant Nadine had the morning to herself and she decided to go to her workroom and do some weaving. It was an art she had learned as a child in Italy and one which had enthralled her ever since. Apart from its practical uses, it was a marvellous therapy if she had anything on her mind. And just recently there had been a number of matters to disturb her normal serenity.

She adored her husband and loved her children and provided all was well with them, especially with Malcolm, nothing else mattered. She had never aspired to be more than a wife and mother. Though intelligent and with an inborn style, militant feminism had no part in her approach to life. From time to time she was required to play hostess at dinner parties, an obligation she undertook without fuss, but equally without enjoyment. Similarly, when she accompanied Malcolm to various functions, she could be charming so that nobody meeting her would guess how tedious she found that aspect of her life.

Though he rarely discussed office matters at home, she knew there were a number that were troubling him. There was his running feud with Adrian Chance, his second partner, which had become a wound that refused to heal. Nadine wasn't in any doubt that Adrian should bow out of the firm and set himself up elsewhere. But there was no sign of that happening. She knew, too, that her husband was more worried than he was prepared to admit about the trouble into which Amanda Ritchie had got herself. But George Ritchie had made a special point of asking him to defend his daughter and he had not felt able to refuse him in view of their long professional association and of the fact that George was a sick man, whose health was a worry in itself. Moreover, Amanda was his godchild. And now there was the complication with Jeremy Scott-Pearce whom Nadine liked and with his father whom she didn't.

They were all matters which had continued to disturb the tranquil atmosphere she tried to create in her home.

There was a knock on the door and Mrs Drake appeared.

"Morning, madam," she said, as she surveyed her employer sitting at her loom. "I always feel music ought to come out of that thing."

"Oh, but it does. Just listen to its soothing sounds."

"I mean proper music. Anyway, sorry if I'm disturbing you, but there's something I think you ought to know. My Pete was in the Queen of Hearts last night and overheard Phil Thorn opening his big mouth. He was saying how he intended getting even with Mr Palfrey."

Nadine frowned. "He was drunk, I expect," she remarked in a tentative voice. "He is most evenings from what I've been told."

Phil Thorn had been the Palfreys' gardener until a month previously when Malcolm Palfrey had fired him for impertinence. He had been remonstrating with Thorn for failing to carry out instructions he had been given about sweeping up leaves from the drive. Thorn had retorted that he had more important things to attend to in the greenhouse and his employer could fetch a rake and get on with his own bloody leaves. Five minutes later he was off the premises, having been told not to re-appear. What really riled him was that he was paid for the exact amount of time he had worked that Saturday morning (it was one hour and twenty minutes) and not a penny more. He had departed fuming with anger and threatening to take his employer before an industrial tribunal. Malcolm Palfrey had treated the threat with contempt which had further incensed Thorn.

Mrs Drake now went on, "There was a bit more to it than that last night. He was talking to that Jacob King who's always being done for poaching and Pete heard him say, 'It'd be easy to make it look like an accident.' This was just after he'd mentioned Mr Palfrey's name."

"Well, thank you for telling me, Mrs Drake," Nadine said after a pause. "I'll certainly pass on what you've told me to my husband."

"Phil Thorn's a good worker, but he's always been a rough-neck," Mrs Drake remarked in a reflective tone. "He had a decent wife until he left her for that Gloria woman and her brood of illegitimate kids. Can't think what men see in her!"

"How many children does she have?"

"Five. All with different fathers." Mrs Drake shook her head uncomprehendingly. "Well, I'd better get on with my work."

For a while Nadine sat staring at her loom. She knew that the likes of Phil Thorn were apt to issue idle threats, particularly in their cups, but it was still unpleasant to be their target.

She heard Maria coming downstairs with Crispin. It was a sunny morning and they'd be going into the garden where her son could amuse himself committing minor mayhem under Maria's indulgent gaze.

She went out into the hall as they reached the bottom of the stairs.

"Keep a good eye on him," she said, addressing Maria in Italian.

Maria looked surprised, then reproachful.

44

"But, of course, signora," she said in a tone that reflected her feeling.

Nadine hadn't intended saying what she had. It had just come out. As she turned to go back to her workroom, the telephone rang. She thought it was probably Malcolm phoning to notify a change in his plans. If so, she hoped it wasn't to say that he would be returning for lunch and bringing someone with him. Naturally she wouldn't demur, but she had fallen into a melancholy mood and would prefer to have the day to herself until Teresa and Cressida came back from school at four-thirty.

"Nettleford four eight two six," she said, with the wariness shown by those who dislike the telephone.

"Nadine, it's Jeremy."

"Jeremy! How lovely to hear your voice. I've been thinking of you so much recently. How are you?"

"All right, but with no thanks to Malcolm. You've presumably heard that he's passed me on to some female solicitor."

"Yes. He says she's very good."

"What else has he said?"

"About what, Jeremy?"

"About the case."

"You know that he doesn't talk shop at home."

"But surely he must have said something about me and Amanda."

"All I know is that he's worried about the case. But that's only natural seeing that it affects people he knows. After all, Amanda is his godchild."

"So I've been reminded at regular intervals. Amanda's one of the reasons I'm calling you, Nadine. Do you know her present address?"

"No. I believe she's staying with friends somewhere in Kent."

"Do you think you could find out for me?"

"I don't see how I can, Jeremy," she said anxiously. "If I asked Malcolm he'd ask why I wished to know."

"Could you find out from the office without Malcolm's knowledge?"

"Miss Seeberg wouldn't tell me, though she'd certainly inform Malcolm that I'd asked." After a pause she went on, "I wish I could help you, Jeremy, but it's not possible."

"I can see it's difficult. I just hoped — "

"I'm really sorry. You know I've always helped you when I can."

"I know. Forget I asked. How are the girls?"

"Both well."

"And young Crispin?"

"Growing rapidly."

He was silent for a moment before speaking again. "Do you have any idea why Amanda has turned against me?"

"I'm sure it's her father's doing. He's a sick man and her arrest came as a great shock to him. It's natural that he looked for someone to blame."

"And I was the obvious fall guy?"

"You must try not to feel bitter, Jeremy. Anyway, who else but Mr Ritchie could have put pressure on Amanda?"

Jeremy decided to leave this question unanswered.

"Well, it's been nice talking to you, Nadine, even if you can't help me. By the way, better not tell Malcolm that we've talked."

"It can be another of our little secrets, *caro* Jeremy."

It was later the same day that Rosa phoned Malcolm Palfrey at his office. They had not been in touch since his visit earlier in the week.

"Hello, Miss Rosa," he said, "I got your message saying you'd take on young Scott-Pearce's defence. I probably ought to have called you back, but I've been up to my eyes with work and I knew you'd get in touch with me in due course."

Rosa swallowed hard to prevent herself making an acerbic comment. He had about as much tact as a rhino in one's back garden.

"I've had a conference with Jeremy," she said, "and you and I must have a talk before the case comes to court."

"I agree, Miss Rosa. We need to get our tackle in order."

"What I need more than anything," Rosa said firmly, "is to know exactly what you're going to say about my client. If you're proposing to throw all the blame on to him, I shall have to refute it."

"Not to worry, Miss Rosa. We'll settle all those details in good time. Leave it to me to have a few words in the right ears."

The thing was, what words? She didn't believe he would wilfully sell her down the river, but she had no great confidence that some of his wheeling-dealing might not put her client at a disadvantage.

"You'll have to excuse me, Miss Rosa," he now went on. "I have an important client waiting to see me. We'll talk again later. I'm sure everything's going to be plain sailing. I'll let the clerk know what we have in mind when I'm in court in the morning. He's a good chap and I'm sure he won't give us any trouble. Just leave it all to me."

Rosa replaced the receiver and stared crossly out of the window at the warehouse wall on the other side of the street. She felt she had been patronised and fobbed off and was near to wishing she had never become involved in the first place. Then she recalled what Robin was fond of saying: "Always remember we're like taxis on a rank waiting for hire. We don't have to like our clients any more than a cab driver has to like his passengers."

Moreover, Jeremy Scott-Pearce (or rather his father) was paying well for her services and she must give him of her best, even if it involved keeping a particularly watchful eye on her co-defender.

Malcolm Palfrey, however, was not the only reason for Rosa feeling out of sorts. She had received a long letter from Peter Chen that morning urging her once more to come and join him in Hong Kong. She and Peter had known one another for nearly four years and been lovers for most of that time. But during the past twelve months Peter had spent more time abroad than in England, most of it in Hong Kong where he had been born and where, with the approach of 1997, family business interests claimed his attention.

He had proposed marriage approximately every six months, but Rosa always countered by pointing out that they were able to enjoy the best of both worlds by not getting wed. But with his continual absence abroad, this no longer held good. She was extremely fond of him and missed him when he was away, but she didn't really see herself as Mrs Chen — or Mrs anyone else for that matter.

Though now thirty-two, she didn't feel ready for marriage. She was sure the day would come, but had no idea when. She did know, however, that when it did she would want to make a full-time commitment to being a wife and mother. She would put the law behind her and throw away her office clothes.

In the meantime, however, Peter was keeping the pressure up. He phoned frequently and wrote her long romantic letters urging her to become his wife. All of which placed Rosa in something of a dilemma, as she didn't want to lose him, nor yet commit herself to marriage. She assumed there were other women in his life, if only on a casual basis, but she didn't know, nor did she wish to be told. Her own life in his absence had become a model of abstinence where sex was concerned.

This morning's letter had said he would be back in London for a few days shortly before Christmas and he suggested they should spend the holiday in Paris or Rome or anywhere Rosa cared to mention. "What about St Moritz?" he had added as a postscript.

Rosa now found herself at once looking forward to his visit and dreading it. During her previous encounter with Malcolm Palfrey, Peter had accompanied her to Nettleford one day and she had introduced the two men to each other. There was instant dislike on both sides.

"He's a charlatan," Peter had later said.

"I suppose there are enough Chinese in London to keep him busy," Malcolm Palfrey had observed the next day in a tone of insufferable superiority.

Rosa had refrained from telling him that Peter made more money than the two of them together and numbered several multi-millionaires amongst his clients, none of them Chinese.

She was sure that, if he had been given the chance, Peter would have advised her against allying herself once more with the solicitor from Nettleford. For that and other less definable reasons she hadn't told him. By the time he arrived back in England, the case should, with luck, be over and she could turn it into an anecdote. That, at any rate, would be her hope.

4

A FEW days later Rosa decided to take matters into her own hands. She had heard nothing further from Malcolm Palfrey and her calls to his office remained unreturned, despite Miss Seeberg's assurances that he was aware that Rosa had been trying to get in touch with him.

"He's been extremely busy, Miss Epton," the secretary said, as though he were the only solicitor in England to whom that applied. "But you can be quite certain he will phone you when he has something to report. There's still a week to go before the case."

A week had now shrunk to five days and Rosa put through a call to the clerk to the justices to ask if she might see him the next afternoon when the court had risen for the day. He had immediately agreed.

"I suppose it's about the case in which you and Mr Palfrey are defending.

Anyway, I'll be glad to meet you."

Douglas Perrick was new to the job since Rosa's previous visit to Nettleford court. He was signing papers when she arrived, but immediately put them on one side.

Leaning back in his chair, he gave her a friendly smile and said, "Well, Miss Epton, what can I do for you? Or have you come to do something for me? Perhaps a bit of both, yes?"

"Probably," Rosa said, returning his smile. "I believe Mr Palfrey has already discussed the case with you — "

"Yes and no," he broke in. "He's mentioned it, but not to any substantive purpose."

"Oh! He told me he was going to speak to you when he was at court earlier this week."

"He didn't turn up. We got a message from his secretary at the last minute saying he had urgent business in London and asking for his case to be adjourned. Since then he hasn't been in touch at all."

"Oh!" Rosa said again in a somewhat nonplussed tone. "I take it, however, you know we're both anxious to have the case dealt with in your court?"

"I wasn't aware any decision had actually been reached on that. Have you approached the prosecution?"

"Not yet."

"I suspect that both they and the police will want it to go to the crown court for trial."

"What about your justices, will they be open to persuasion?"

The clerk placed his hands together and rested the point of his chin on his fingertips.

"It's not for me to prejudge their decision, Miss Epton."

"I realise that."

"Nevertheless, my view is that they could be persuaded to deal with the case if both sides were agreeable. Even though," he went on slowly, "there's certain pressure on them not to deal with it summarily."

"I'm told," Rosa said in a carefully neutral tone, "that Mr Anstey mightn't favour that course."

"And Mr Anstey is a near neighbour of Mr Churchman who is chairman of our bench. Though I understand," he added drily, "that they are not on particularly neighbourly terms."

Rosa took a deep breath. "I wouldn't attempt to deny that what my client and his co-defendant did was both foolish and criminal and could have had disastrous consequences. In essence, however, it was no more than a stupid prank committed by two young people who were obviously under the influence of drink at the time and who didn't pause to consider the possible dangers."

"I gather from what you've just said that they're proposing to plead guilty?"

Rosa looked at the clerk in surprise.

"Certainly. Hadn't Mr Palfrey told you that?"

"Not in so many words. He had merely mentioned it as one of the options under consideration."

"I can see that your justices mightn't be too keen to try it as a contested case, but if they agree to deal with it on the basis of a plea of guilty, it will save everyone time and expense."

The clerk nodded judicially. "And since I'm always complaining about defendants who waste court time by seeking trial in the crown court for some petty offence, it hardly becomes me to sing a different song to you." He went on in a thoughtful tone, "I suppose putting a lighted firework through a letter box isn't the most serious crime in the calendar, though I can think of a few judges I've known who'd regard it as a matter for thunderous denunciation."

"No one's suggesting it was done with an intent to endanger life."

"Frankly, I'm surprised the prosecution hasn't preferred such a charge, if only as a bargaining counter."

"They could never prove it."

"That wouldn't prevent them making it. But they haven't, so we needn't consider hypothetical situations."

"So if everyone agrees, the case can be disposed of next Thursday?" Rosa said.

"I'd understood a further remand would be asked for," the clerk said in surprise.

"If it's a plea of guilty, why can't the matter be concluded there and then?" Rosa urged.

"Can I assume you're speaking for

57

Malcolm Palfrey as well as yourself."

Rosa bit her lip. "All I can say is that we've discussed the case and it was my understanding that your court would be asked to deal with it on the basis of a plea of guilty. Moreover, I thought Mr Palfrey had spoken to you on those lines."

"Well, he hasn't. He may have intended to do so but, as I mentioned, he wasn't in court on Tuesday and his case was put over." He reached for his telephone. "Let's see if we can get him in his office, shall we?"

But Malcolm Palfrey was out and Miss Seeberg was vague about his movements.

"Well, there's only one thing we can do, Miss Epton, I'll have a word with the chairman of the justices and you'd better get hold of Malcolm Palfrey and secure his confirmation of the proposed course of action. And you'd also better have a talk with the crown prosecutor's office."

"I'll do that immediately."

"Otherwise, he'll turn up unprepared. Not that there would be anything unusual in that! He has half the staff he's supposed to have and more case files than he can count. You should be able to get him on your side without too much difficulty. The poor chap jumps at anything that'll lead to a quieter life."

"I'm very grateful to you," Rosa said standing up. "It's been a most helpful discussion. We'll meet in court on Thursday."

"Fingers crossed," the clerk remarked with a smile.

The crown prosecution solicitor to whom Rosa spoke the next day proved immediately amenable to her suggested course of action.

"There's only one thing, Miss Epton," he said in a worried voice. "I don't know whether I'll be able to serve any statements on you by then. I'd not reckoned on such a quick disposal."

"I'm not too concerned about that," Rosa replied. "Tell me, though, do they contain anything that might take me by surprise?"

"I don't think so. Apart from Mr Anstey's statement, it's police and scientific evidence."

"Scientific?"

"About the type of firework and the

damage it caused. I gather the rug is beyond repair and Mr Anstey values it at two thousand pounds. Incidentally, he's not going to like the case being dealt with summarily."

"Provided the prosecution and defence agree and the court's amenable, Mr Anstey can foam at the mouth for all I care. He's not in control of the case."

"No, of course not. But . . . well, I hope, he won't create too much of a fuss."

"I'm sure you won't let yourself be pressurised," Rosa said firmly.

"Certainly not," he replied as though Rosa had given him an untimely jab in the ribs.

After ringing off she decided it was time to let Malcolm Palfrey know what she had been up to. She hoped he would be fully approving, but was less than sure about this.

"I was just about to call you, Miss Rosa," he said when they were connected.

"As I hadn't heard from you and as time was running out, I've been in touch with the clerk of the court and also with the prosecuting solicitor. As a result, it looks as if the case can be dealt with next Thursday on the basis of a plea of guilty."

For a moment, there was silence at the other end of the line, then Malcolm Palfrey said, "I hope I can be ready in time."

"How do you mean?"

"I have to obtain some further details from my client and there's also a question of deciding what witnesses to call to back up my plea in mitigation. I'll do my best, but I'm not making any promises. In any event, what's the urgency?"

"But I thought it was what we'd agreed," Rosa expostulated.

"Trouble is, I've been very much occupied with other matters, which have taken priority over everything else."

"In my view," Rosa said firmly, "it's in the interests of both our clients to have the case over and done with as soon as possible."

"Another week or so isn't going to blight their lives. If I may say so, Miss Rosa, I wish you'd had a word with me before dashing off to see Perrick and speaking to the prosecution."

"It wasn't for want of trying," Rosa said crossly.

"I did tell you that I had everything in hand. Now you've made me look a bit foolish with Douglas Perrick."

"That certainly wasn't my intention and I don't believe it's the case. I've not acted behind your back."

"That's a matter of opinion. This is my neck of the woods and it would have been better if you hadn't come barging in the way you did."

Rosa found herself almost speechless with indignation. She had phoned, expecting to receive at least a measure of thanks for what she had accomplished, instead of which she was being berated for having acted like a tiresome busybody. For two pins, she'd tell Malcolm Palfrey he could have back the client he had foisted on her. That, however, would hardly be fair on Jeremy Scott-Pearce who was in no way to blame for what was happening.

She was frankly bewildered by Palfrey's reaction and could only conclude that she had managed to wound him deeply where it hurt most, namely his vanity. But that was entirely his own fault. A single phone call from him could have prevented the present contretemps. She was damned if she was going to apologise.

Making a considerable effort to keep her voice under control, she said, "We still need to discuss what we're going to tell the court about the apportionment of blame for what happened. Jeremy denies absolutely that he was solely responsible."

"I play these things by ear," he said loftily. "If I say anything with which you disagree, you can tell the court."

Rosa bit her lip. He really was being most contrary. In the circumstances there seemed to be little point in continuing the conversation.

"Well, I'll see you in court next Thursday," she said crisply. "And I hope we don't hit any further snags."

"The man's a charlatan," had been Peter Chen's judgment of Malcolm Palfrey. On today's evidence he was a mixture of prima donna and bear with a sore head.

Rosa was baffled.

5

SHE phoned Jeremy Scott-Pearce from home that evening and asked him to come to the office the next day.

"Has something come up?" he asked with what Rosa thought was undue suspicion.

"No, but there are still one or two 't's to cross and 'i's' to dot before we get to court."

"OK, when shall I come?"

The appointment was made and Rosa decided that when she saw him she would put a gloss on what had happened with Malcolm Palfrey. She didn't wish to upset him just before the case. It was one thing to get a client to face reality, another to arouse unnecessary anxiety. It was up to her to cope with Malcolm Palfrey when the time came.

"Will you be driving to Nettleford on the morning?" she asked as he prepared to leave on conclusion of their conference.

He frowned as though the question had hidden significance. "I expect so. Why do you ask?"

"I can offer you a lift if it's any help."

"Oh, I see. I'll manage. Thanks all the same."

"When are you expecting your father?"

"I've told him I don't want him to come to court. Don't get me wrong! I'm still grateful for his support, but I don't want him sitting there breathing down my neck. I've said he's welcome to sit outside if he wants, but not to show his face until it's all over." He grimaced. "I may need him then to pay the fine."

From what Rosa knew of Mr Scott-Pearce, he was unlikely to accept being consigned to the shadows.

"Get to court in good time," she said as she rose to see him out. "We may need to have some last-minute words."

He reached the door and paused. Then in a curiously brittle tone, he said, "Has Malcolm Palfrey spoken about me recently?"

"He's not said anything I've not told you. I've had very little contact with him since you were last here. He seems to have been exceptionally busy and I've had difficulty getting hold of him. Anyway, were you expecting him to have said something about you?"

Jeremy shrugged. "I just wondered, that's all." He gave her a flip of his hand. "See you on Thursday."

Rosa gazed after his retreating back as she wondered what had prompted his question. She was sure it wasn't as casual as he pretended. She had nearly asked him if he had succeeded in getting in touch with Amanda, but had then decided it was better she shouldn't know. Sometimes information could prove an embarrassment.

Two days later she got up rather earlier than usual and after a breakfast consisting of her usual cup of black coffee, augmented always on the days she was appearing in court by a slice of toast and honey, she got into her small Honda and threaded her way out of town through the early morning traffic, most of which was heading in the opposite direction.

She reached Nettleford in just over an

hour, though the journey seemed much longer than that. She parked in the market place, where a clock showed the time as being five minutes before nine. The court didn't sit till ten and there was no guarantee that her case would come on immediately. How long it would last was anyone's guess. That would largely depend on how expansive the prosecuting solicitor decided to be, and on the verbal flow of Malcolm Palfrey's advocacy.

As she locked her car and glanced about her, she observed the familiar figure of Miss Seeberg hurrying along the pavement on the further side of the square. To Rosa it was an opportunity to find out when Malcolm Palfrey was likely to arrive and whether his threat about not being ready was still a reality.

Hurrying across the road to head off the secretary, Rosa was impressed by the speed with which Miss Seeberg was moving. She was like a galleon under full sail in a strong wind and Rosa was obliged to break into a run in order to confront her.

"Good morning, Miss Seeberg," she said somewhat breathlessly, "I saw you as I was getting out of my car."

The secretary looked momentarily indignant as though nobody had any right to be in her path. Then her expression cleared.

"It's Miss Epton, isn't it? I'm afraid I didn't recognise you at first." She appeared hot and flustered. "I was hurrying as I'm late. So if you'll excuse me."

"I want to have a word with Mr Palfrey before the court sits. Are you expecting him in the office first?"

"Yes, but he has an appointment. I'll let him know you wish to speak to him."

"As far as you know, is he ready to go ahead with the case?"

"I know nothing to the contrary, Miss Epton," Miss Seeberg remarked in a tone of chilly reproof.

"That's fine then. I think I'll go and have a cup of coffee in the County Hotel until it's time to go across to court."

Rosa found a table in the bay window of the hotel's lounge from where she was able to observe everything that was going on outside. As she sat sipping a cup of lukewarm coffee, she noticed a Volvo Estate car pull into a parking space. A girl got out of the back and from the driver's seat emerged a stoutish woman in a suede jacket. The two women then assisted a frail-looking man get out of the front passenger seat. He was muffled up against the cold east wind and leaned heavily on the older woman's arm as they moved off. Rosa felt sure they must be the Ritchies, father, mother and daughter, Amanda. From the direction in which they went, she guessed they were on their way to Malcolm Palfrey's office. Miss Seeberg had mentioned he had an appointment and the Ritchies were his obvious visitors. She assumed that Palfrey had by now arrived at his office and she recalled that he used to park his car in a small yard at the rear.

Some fifteen minutes later, a red sports car made a noisy arrival in the square and Rosa hurried out of the hotel to intercept her client before he could disappear.

"Hi there, Jeremy," she called out as she weaved her way between parked vehicles.

He turned and gave her a hollow-eyed look.

"Oh, hello," he said dully.

"Have you just arrived from town?"

He nodded. He looked anything but well and in addition had managed to cut himself shaving, so that he had a battle-weary expression.

"Are you feeling all right?" Rosa asked a shade anxiously.

He shook his head. "I feel awful. I hardly slept last night. I think it must have been something I ate."

Rosa gazed at him thoughtfully for a moment or two. "We'd better find a chemist," she said. "They'll mix you something which'll settle your stomach." He looked reluctant and she went on. "There's nothing worse than being stuck in court with a heaving tummy." As they walked across to a row of shops she said, "I think I saw the Ritchies arrive. They've gone to Mr Palfrey's office."

"I think I'm going to throw up," he said suddenly and dived through the door of a public toilet which, by good fortune, they happened to be passing.

Rosa walked on a few yards and

pretended to interest herself in an estate agent's window. Jeremy reappeared after about five minutes. He still looked awful and she wondered whether an adjournment mightn't be necessary. Admittedly on a plea of guilty he would have nothing to do save sit and listen; even so he should be able to show an intelligent interest in the proceedings. At the moment he looked quite incapable of taking an interest in anything.

They found a chemist's shop and Rosa spoke to a white-coated dispenser who nodded sagely and produced a medicine glass of clouded liquid, which Jeremy dutifully drank.

"It's never failed yet," the dispenser said cheerfully. "But if he's not feeling better in a few hours, he'd better see a doctor."

As they left the shop Rosa said, "Let's go across to the court. You can sit quietly until the case comes on." She hoped that the chemist's confidence in his mixture would shortly manifest itself For the time being she didn't wish to put the idea into her client's head that the case could be postponed. She was gazing at him doubtfully when an usher came over.

"Miss Epton? Mr Perrick would like to have a word with you. He's in court."

Court-rooms before the start of a case always reminded Rosa of the sort of modern play in which small groups of people sit or stand around making desultory conversation while waiting for something significant to happen.

The clerk was talking to a female colleague when Rosa approached and gave her a friendly smile. Two or three other people were lounging in seats later to be occupied by press or public.

"All set to go?" Mr Perrick asked.

"My client isn't feeling terribly well, but I think he'll be all right. It's something he ate last night."

"Or drank perhaps?" Perrick observed drily. "Defendants are liable to have a night out before they appear in court. I suppose they think it may be their last opportunity for some time." He glanced around the nearly empty courtroom. "Well, once Mr Pearman from the CPS arrives and Mr Palfrey crosses the road from his office, we can begin. I'm not anticipating any problems.

"Mr Anstey hasn't tried to throw any spanners in the works?" Rosa said.

"Oh, he's tried all right, but his efforts haven't got him anywhere. Upholding the law and bowing to Mr Anstey's wishes aren't necessarily the same thing."

"I'll go and wait with my client," Rosa said, relieved by what she had heard.

She returned to find Jeremy sitting where she had left him. He still looked wretched and he shook his head when Rosa enquired if he was feeling any better.

"We should be able to start fairly soon," she said. "Any sign of your father?"

"No, I told you — "

"Yes, I know. I just wondered if he'd looked in?" As she spoke she glanced across at the main entrance. Giving Jeremy a nudge she said, "Aren't those the Ritchies coming in now?"

"Yes," he said, looking up with reluctance.

"Who's the man with them?" Rosa asked in a puzzled tone.

"That's Adrian Chance. He's Malcolm's partner.

Rosa frowned as she watched Chance disappear inside the court. Meanwhile the Ritchies were holding a whispered conversation and displaying signs of agitation.

The same usher now approached Rosa again and said the clerk would like to speak to her again. She followed him across the lobby and into court.

"We seem to have hit a snag," the clerk said as Rosa came up to where he and Adrian Chance were talking. "Mr Palfrey's gone missing. Incidentally, this is his partner, Mr Chance." Adrian Chance gave Rosa a curt nod and Perrick went on, "He hasn't turned up at his office this morning and it appears he didn't spend last night at home. Mr Chance has spoken to Mrs Palfrey on the phone and she says he went out just before nine yesterday evening and never came back. She's naturally very worried about him. His secretary has phoned round the local hospitals and spoken to the police, but has been unable to find out anything."

"I should think he's had some sort of brainstorm and will be found wandering around with a loss of memory," Adrian Chance said. He seemed to regard his partner's disappearance as more of an irritation than a cause for anxiety. "You'd better adjourn the case."

"You can't do it for him?" Rosa said. "After all, it *is* a plea of guilty."

"Impossible," he said, shaking his head. "It's Palfrey's case and the Ritchies are entitled to have his services, provided they're available."

"Perhaps if we give him another half hour, he may turn up," the clerk said.

"That's up to you," Chance replied briskly.

At that moment a figure came hurrying into court, looking as though he'd run from the other side of town.

"Sorry I'm late," he said as he gasped for breath. "I'm afraid my car broke down."

"This is Mr Pearman from the CPS," the clerk said and went on to tell the prosecuting solicitor what had happened.

"It's nice to know that, for once, I'm not to blame," Pearman remarked amiably.

Perrick turned back to Chance. "Maybe

your office will have learnt something by now?"

"Miss Seeberg would have phoned if there was any news," he said. "But I'll get back to the office, anyway. Nothing I can do by hanging about here."

Perrick glanced at his watch. "It's only just after ten. Why don't we review the situation again at, say, eleven o'clock. If Mr Palfrey hasn't turned up by then, there'll have to be an adjournment." He gave Rosa a wry look. "Always fatal to think something's going to be trouble-free in our job."

But eleven o'clock came without any sign of Malcolm Palfrey. Though by the merest coincidence it was near enough the hour when his body was discovered on a park bench some eight miles from Nettleford. A revolver lay beside him and he had a bullet wound in the head.

6

THE park at Shilman Green was a precious five acres of green turf, adorned by a number of oak and chestnut trees and several large clumps of shrubs. An asphalt path ran more or less diagonally from the entrance in Station Road to a wicket gate set in the hawthorn hedge which bounded the farther side. From there the path passed through a small wood to emerge at the northern side of a new housing estate populated by yuppies and their successors.

In the farthest corner of the park was a small secluded area known locally as Pan's Place. It consisted of a three-quarter circle of rhododendron bushes within whose confines were set three wooden benches. In the very middle stood a small statue of the god Pan. Seeing that amongst other things he was the deity of pastures and woods, his presence was not entirely inappropriate.

From time to time the parish council

77

held heated debates about Pan's Place. Some argued that it was an invitation to licentious behaviour; others, more liberally disposed, said nonsense and words to that effect. So far this second faction had won the day, but it only needed to become the scene of a rape for the benches to be removed and the screen of rhododendrons to be uprooted. What would happen to Pan was anybody's guess.

Tom Berry, the park-keeper, had mixed feelings about the area. Being only twenty-five, he was all in favour of young people having somewhere quiet and secluded to sit on a summer's evening, but clearing up after them was a less agreeable chore and one that he always left to the end.

On a Thursday in early December, however, he didn't expect to find anything worse than the pile of fallen leaves that the wind invariably deposited at Pan's feet.

As he approached Pan's Place he saw a pair of legs sticking out from one of the seats. He at once assumed that they belonged to a vagrant who had chosen to spend the night there. It was a not unknown occurrence.

But as he pushed his way through the opening between the rhododendrons, there came into view the body of a respectably dressed man slumped on one of the benches. There was dried blood round a hole in his right temple and a revolver lay on the ground as if it had fallen from his hand.

Only six months earlier Tom had been a medical student. He was used to seeing dead bodies and had no feelings of revulsion or panic. For a full minute he stared at the scene, taking in all its detail. He knew that he must preserve it until the police arrived. If he went for help himself, there was always the chance that some kid might stumble on the scene. It was obvious that none of the morning commuters on their way across the park to the station had strayed that far from the path.

He spent another half minute looking about him before parting the bushes and leaving Pan's Place.

It was a cold, grey day and the park was deserted apart from an old lady in the distance who was throwing sticks for a small, energetic dog and a boy riding a bicycle on the path toward Station Road. Tom recognised the rider as the delivery boy for George Blatchington and Son, family butcher. He gave him a shout. The boy stopped and looked in Tom's direction. Bicycles were not allowed to be ridden in the park and Tom could see what was going on in the lad's mind.

"I need your help," Tom called out and began to run towards him.

"What do you want?" the boy asked with a mixture of suspicion and aggression. "I'm not doing anything wrong."

"I want you to go and phone the police. It's urgent."

"The police. What for?"

"There's a body over in Pan's Place."

"What sort of body?" the boy asked with a deepening frown.

"A man's body. It looks as though he's shot himself By the way, what's your name?"

"Gavin."

"Well, look, Gavin, go back to the shop and phone the police. Say that Tom Berry, the park-keeper, has found a body and that I'm staying here to preserve the scene until they come. Will you do that . . . now . . . without delay?"

"Suppose I couldn't have a look first?"

Tom hesitated. It wasn't so long ago that he had been a boy himself and well . . .

"OK, but let's be quick about it."

Propping his bicycle against a tree, Gavin broke into a trot at Tom's side.

"Sure you still want to take a look?" Tom asked when they reached Pan's Place. The boy bit his lip and nodded. "Don't go beyond the entrance or you'll be in trouble with the police."

Gavin moved forward cautiously as though treading on thin ice. He peered into Pan's Place, then suddenly turned and said in a hoarse voice, "I know who he is. He's a lawyer from Nettleford."

"How do you know that?"

"He's Mr Blatchington's solicitor and comes into the shop when he's after something a bit special like Scotch fillet of steak or our home-made sausages." He gave Tom a bewildered, half-frightened look. "What's happened? What's he doing here?"

"That'll be for the police to find out,

so off you go and fetch help."

Tom watched him run back to where he had left his cycle and pedal down the path as if the hound of the Baskervilles was on his tail.

What, indeed, Tom wondered, had a respectable local solicitor been doing in Pan's Place on a winter's night? He decided to take a further look at the scene of the lawyer's death. After that he sat down on the ground where he could see the whole park and awaited the arrival of the police. He fell to wondering what Pan could tell them if he were able to speak.

The next couple of hours passed in a kaleidoscope of activity as police and others came and departed. Pan's Place was screened off so that their work could proceed away from curious eyes. Tom, however, was allowed to remain out of deference to his official status. He observed the comings and goings with interest, even if he viewed with despair the cars, vans and motor-cycles that charged across the green turf, leaving deep scars wherever they went.

One of the cars brought Detective

Chief Inspector Harshaw to the scene. He introduced himself to Tom and listened to his account of his discovery of the body with close attention. Later he commended him for the action he had taken.

Later still when a dank mist began rising from the ground, the area was sealed off and everyone departed, leaving Pan to keep a lonely vigil.

As DCI Harshaw drove away, he knew that his own day was only just beginning. It certainly had the appearance of a case of suicide, but why should Malcolm Palfrey, whom he knew personally and didn't regard as the type to take his life, suddenly shoot himself? Or, more to the point, if he wanted to commit suicide, why choose Pan's Place as the setting?

He hoped the autopsy would settle the basic issue of suicide or murder, but either way there were going to be a lot of questions requiring answers before the enquiry was finally concluded.

He determined in the meantime to keep an open mind. The first person to interview would be Mrs Palfrey. Thereafter he would just have to follow his nose. He hoped that, with luck, the next few hours would establish whether he had to look for a murderer or whether the Nettleford solicitor had succumbed to some intolerable pressure and taken his life.

He had only just left the scene when a radio message informed him that the revolver found by the body was Palfrey's own property and was duly recorded in the weapon register at Nettleford police station.

That seemed to point to suicide, though it didn't explain why he had chosen such an improbable place to kill himself

7

NEWS can often travel with the speed of light. Particularly bad news, which is frequently embellished by the lively imagination of its purveyors.

Thus it was that the wife of one of the partners in a rival firm of solicitors, who happened to be buying *escalopes* of veal in George Blatchington's butcher's shop, overheard the phone call to the police. She drove back to Nettleford at breakneck speed and rushed into her husband's office to announce breathlessly that Malcolm Palfrey had blown his brains out.

Her husband immediately phoned Adrian Chance and was given extremely short shrift. Nevertheless, Chance felt obliged to phone the police station where he was told in guarded terms that a body bearing gunshot wounds had been discovered in the park at Shilman Green. As yet it had not been formally identified, but there was reason to think it might be Malcolm Palfrey.

Chance immediately left for court, though before doing so, he poked his head round the door of Miss Seeberg's office.

"I'm afraid there may be bad news about Mr Palfrey," he said in a grim voice.

"I knew it," Miss Seeberg exclaimed. "He's dead, isn't he? I knew something awful would happen."

Chance forbore to probe her immediate assumption. Informing her where he was going, he left her staring into space with an anguished expression.

On arrival at court he noticed Amanda Ritchie and Jeremy Scott-Pearce talking earnestly in a corner of the lobby but, ignoring them, he dashed through the swing doors to find Perrick, the clerk, Rosa and the prosecuting solicitor conversing together. Mr and Mrs Ritchie sat near by.

"I've just received news which suggests that Malcolm Palfrey is dead," he announced in a portentous tone. "I'm expecting confirmation from the police at any moment. Somebody's been found shot dead in the park over at Shilman Green and it would appear to be Palfrey. I can't tell you anything more at this stage."

"I know that he's been somewhat worried of late," Mr Ritchie remarked. "He phoned me a couple of times about Amanda and mentioned that he had problems on his mind."

"Did he say what problems?" Chance asked sharply.

"No. And, of course, I didn't ask."

"Well, for everyone's sake, let's hope it was suicide and not murder," Perrick remarked.

"I'm not sure that I go along with that sentiment," Chance retorted. "Suicide can do considerably more harm to the firm than a murder investigation." Observing the expressions of those around him he went on, "If it's suicide, it'll be assumed that the answer lies somewhere in our files and ledgers."

Mr Ritchie turned his head away in apparent distaste at this view.

Rosa had listened in attentive silence to what was said. Malcolm Palfrey's death, be it suicide or murder, was a wholly unforeseen development and she found herself cold-bloodedly wishing that it could have been postponed for twenty-four hours. By then the case would have been over and she would have had no need to do anything more than write a letter of sympathy to Nadine Palfrey. As it was, she could see herself caught in something of a dilemma.

A minute or two later one of Mr Perrick's staff came into court and said the police had confirmed that the dead man was Malcolm Palfrey and that he had apparently died from a gunshot wound to the head. A full autopsy was due to be conducted later that day. Meanwhile, Detective Chief Inspector Harshaw would be grateful if anyone who had information that might be relevant would get in touch with him. He understood that Mr Palfrey had been due to appear in a case that morning.

Rosa decided it was time to go in search of Jeremy. She found him sitting on his own in the lobby staring into space.

"How much longer do I have to stay

here?" he asked tetchily.

"I'm sorry, I didn't realise you were in a hurry to leave. When I last spoke to you, you said you were feeling better."

"That doesn't mean I want to hang around here for the rest of the day."

Rosa sighed. "You can leave any time you want," she said. "The case has been adjourned and you've been granted bail. If I'd realised you were in a hurry . . . " She gave a shrug. "In the event, however, I'm glad you have stayed. I'm afraid there's bad news about Mr Palfrey. He's been found dead in a park. We've just heard."

"Suicide, was it?" he asked awkwardly.

"All I know is that he had a gunshot wound to the head. I don't even know whether there was a weapon to suggest that he had killed himself."

"He had a nine millimetre Browning automatic. He'd had it since he was a colonel in the Territorial Army. Lots of people knew he had it. There was no secret about it." He paused and gave Rosa a resigned look. "It would be my guess that he shot himself because he couldn't face life any longer."

"I suggest you keep your views to yourself," Rosa said firmly. "You certainly don't want to stick your neck out. Remember the case isn't over yet, it's only been adjourned."

"Amanda thinks they'll drop it."

"I can't see why they should. After all, lawyers are not irreplaceable." Rosa was thoughtful for a moment. "If the police should approach you, refer them to me. I'll be in touch with developments and be ready to play it by ear. At the moment there's nothing any of us can do until it's been established how he died."

"I think I ought to call on Nadine on my way home."

"I strongly advise against that. The police are sure to be there and your presence won't be welcome. You can phone her from home this evening if you want to speak to her."

"She's a lovely person."

"Maybe, but it's still not the moment to go visiting." Rosa glanced round the almost deserted lobby. "Incidentally, has your father shown up?"

"He phoned the court office to say he had to return to Geneva on urgent business and couldn't get here. He told them he would meet any fine or costs."

It struck Rosa as regrettable that business took precedence over his son's fate in court, but she refrained from comment.

"Well, I'm off," Jeremy said, getting up. He paused and shrugged. "Poor old Malcolm!"

Rosa watched him cross the lobby and disappear through the main door. What a mixed-up young man he was! Spoilt and petulant and patently insecure, though not without a certain charm.

She crossed her fingers that Malcolm Palfrey's death would not seriously involve her in its aftermath. The last thing she wanted was to become embroiled in a police investigation, though she now accepted as inevitable that they would wish to interview her and her young client.

After all, whether he had died by his own hand or that of another, his life was bound to come under intense scrutiny.

There would be questions that demanded answers.

8

"ARE you quite sure, Mrs Palfrey, that your husband gave no indication where he was going when he left home yesterday evening?"

It was a question DCI Harshaw kept coming back to, though receiving a negative answer each time. The trouble was that he hadn't yet made up his mind whether he believed her. He didn't think she was deliberately lying, nevertheless he had the impression she wasn't being as frank as she might be.

They were sitting in the drawing-room at Kingsmere Farm. A composed Nadine sat facing him and Woman Police Constable Perkins. Nadine seemed numbed by the news of her husband's death, but remained in control of her emotions. Harshaw, who thought all Italians screamed and shouted and flung their arms about, had expected a flood of tears and streams of denunciation. He was unaware of her strong strain of Slav blood which made her less volatile and more deeply brooding.

"Didn't you ask him where he was going?"

"If he'd wanted me to know, he'd have told me."

"Did he often go out at night like that?"

"Not often, but sometimes."

"Tell me exactly what he said when he left."

"That he had to meet somebody, but hoped not to be long."

"Did you think he might be going to his office?"

"It was possible."

"Was he always as mysterious about his comings and goings?"

"Solicitors often have to meet clients out of office hours."

"So you believed he was going to meet a client?"

"It was possible," she said again and gave a graphic shrug.

"Did you know that he took a revolver with him?"

"No."

"Had you ever known him to go out armed like that?"

She made a helpless gesture. "How would I know unless he told me?"

"Had he ever talked about suicide?"

"He was not the type to kill himself," she said firmly.

"Supposing he did take his own life, can you think of any reason?"

She shook her head and Harshaw continued. "Had he been depressed of late?"

"He worked too hard."

"Did that depress him?"

"It made him irritable, but not for long.

"Was he a good husband and father?"

"Yes."

"Do you know whether he had any particular office problems?"

Nadine frowned. "Don't all offices create problems?"

"Probably, but I'm only interested in Palfrey and Co. at the moment."

"You must speak to his partner, Mr Chance."

"I gather his secretary had been with him a long time . . . I've heard rumours that she was in love with your husband."

Nadine gave a small laugh. "A lot of secretaries are secretly in love with their employers. Malcolm was a very attractive man, but I'm sure he never did anything to encourage Miss Seeberg."

Perhaps that was the trouble, Harshaw reflected.

"Can you think of anyone who had a grudge against your husband?"

"Only a man named Thorn. He was our gardener until my husband gave him the sack. Mrs Drake, who cleans for me, mentioned the other day that her husband had overheard Thorn talking in the pub. He heard Thorn and the other man mention my husband's name and Thorn said that it would be easy to make it look like an accident."

"Make what look like an accident?" Harshaw asked while WPC Perkins scribbled in her notebook.

"My husband's death. What else?"

"I also assumed that, but I wanted to be sure we were understanding one another." He paused. "I think that's all for the moment, Mrs Palfrey. As soon as I have the results of the post mortem examination and of various scientific tests, I'll be in touch with you again. Meanwhile, thank you for being so helpful."

As they drove away from the house, WPC Perkins said, "I didn't think she was particularly helpful, sir."

"Nor did I. The point is, was she being deliberately evasive or did she genuinely not know all the answers?"

"In my view, sir, she was, to use the now well-used phrase, being economical with the truth." They reached the road which ran at the end of the drive. "Where to now, sir?"

"To the deceased's office," Harshaw replied, giving her a speculative glance. He'd probably find out she had a degree in English literature. You just didn't know these days, when PCs pounding the beat could be doctors of philosophy.

★ ★ ★

As they pulled up outside the solicitor's office, Detective Sergeant Whitehead materialised on the pavement alongside.

"We've found Palfrey's car," he

announced. "It was parked in a lane about a quarter of a mile from the park. It's being gone over for fingerprints. No sign of any farewell messages in it to say what Palfrey was up to."

Harshaw winced. He deplored the sergeant's brash and flippant manner which grated on him. He himself made a point of being courteous to everyone with whom he came into contact and treated all and sundry with respect, with the possible exception of those who preyed on the old and the young.

"Was it locked?" he asked.

"Yes. We found the keys, you remember, in Palfrey's jacket pocket."

Harshaw did remember. Glancing across at the building outside which they had stopped, he said, "I'm about to interview Mr Palfrey's partner and his secretary."

"I don't know if it's struck your notice, guvnor, but the station car park is right next door to the other park and yet our dead friend left his car some distance away where it'd be unlikely to be noticed."

Harshaw nodded. "Yes, I had noticed. One would like to know why. Meanwhile, tell Dr Rudd that I'd be grateful for a word with him when he's completed the PM. Ask him not to rush off before I get to the mortuary."

"Will do," Whitehead said, withdrawing his head from the open car window. WPC Perkins who had been quietly holding her breath now began breathing normally again. She was a fastidious girl and disliked blasts of other people's breath in her face. She found Sergeant Whitehead's particularly obnoxious.

As they got out of the car, Harshaw was aware of Adrian Chance observing their arrival from an upstairs window. He ducked out of sight as soon as the Chief Inspector looked up. A few minutes later they were being shown into his office.

"So what have you to tell me?" the solicitor enquired stiffly.

"I'm hoping, Mr Chance, that it's you who have things to tell me. Why, for example, should Mr Palfrey have committed suicide — "

"So it *is* suicide," Chance interrupted in a grim tone.

"Or who might have wished to murder him?" Harshaw went on.

"You mean you don't know which it was?"

"I'm hoping the PM report will help as to that, though I'm less sanguine than I was. Let's assume for a moment that it was suicide, what reason might Mr Palfrey have had for taking his life?"

"I've spoken to the bank and had a quick look through our ledgers, but I can find no suggestion that he's misused clients' money."

"You've already checked that?" Harshaw said in some surprise.

"I felt it my duty to do so, as I knew you were sure to ask."

"Did the speed with which you acted indicate suspicion on your part?"

"Certainly not, but I wanted to satisfy myself that nothing was amiss."

"And your quick check has put your mind at rest on that score?"

"On the face of it no money has been misappropriated."

"But you'd hardly expect such a superficial check to reveal deep-seated fraud, would you? I mean, the sort of check you've made is no more than counting one's change after making a purchase. Am I right?"

"Obviously I've not had time to make a full check," Chance retorted with a note of indignation. "All I'm saying is that I don't believe the answer to his death lies in this office." He paused and went on. "Personally, I don't believe he did kill himself I think it's much more likely he was murdered."

"I'd like to hear your theory about that," Harshaw said, leaning forward with an interested expression.

"In the first place, Palfrey was far too much of an extrovert to commit suicide. Secondly, the circumstances of his death seem to make suicide highly improbable. Why choose that particular spot to blow out his brains when he could have done it much nearer home and saved himself a journey?"

It seemed to Harshaw that Palfrey and Co.'s surviving partner was being unnecessarily callous. Though it was common knowledge in the police that the two men didn't get on, he had not expected it to be made so obvious.

"So who do you think killed him?" he asked.

"I've no idea. Presumably it was the person he went to meet. Mrs Palfrey told me he left home around nine to go and meet someone."

"That is what he said, which isn't the same thing. He might not have intended meeting *anyone*. But to get back to who might have killed him, do you have anyone in mind?"

"Palfrey wasn't short of enemies, but you'd hardly expect me to give you a list of names."

"I'm sure you want to do all you can to assist my enquiry and if you know of anyone who had a motive to kill him, I'd like to hear it."

"It could be worth your while to question Phil Thorn."

"The ex-gardener?"

"Yes. I understand he'd been uttering threats against Palfrey in a pub."

"Anyone else?"

"No."

"But you said just now he had a lot of enemies — "

"There were a lot of people who didn't

like him, but that doesn't make them murderers."

"Would you put yourself in that category?"

Chance glared at him. "With the greatest respect, Chief Inspector, that's an impertinent question."

"I'll try not to offend you again, but I can't guarantee it. Meanwhile, I'd like to talk to Miss Seeberg."

"I sent her home. She was so upset by Palfrey's death that I told her to take the afternoon off. I'm sure she'll be back in the morning, so you can interview her then."

Harshaw gave a nod as if agreeing to the suggestion. A few minutes later he and WPC Perkins returned to their car.

"Are we going back to the station, sir?" she asked. She had originally been asked to accompany him as she might be needed to offer comfort and support to Malcolm Palfrey's grieving widow. That had not proved necessary and she had expected to be dropped off at the station on their return to Nettleford, but Harshaw seemed to have other ideas.

"No, we're going to visit Miss Seeberg

102

at home," he said with a small smile. "I have an idea she was kept out of our way and I want to find out why."

"Do we know her address, sir?"

"We shall do as soon as you get on the blower and ask."

★ ★ ★

Madge Seeberg wasn't only upset, she was extremely annoyed. She had known that the police were sure to visit the office that afternoon and she had wanted to be there to have her say. But Mr Chance had insisted that she go home and had bundled her into the taxi which he had ordered.

Since getting back she had drunk six cups of tea and even smoked several cigarettes, something she did only on the rarest of occasions. She was on the point of making a further pot of tea when she saw the car pull up outside and DCI Harshaw get out, followed by a young woman whom she had not previously seen. She arrived at the front door before they reached it and stood waiting for them.

"I'm sorry to bother you at home, Miss Seeberg. May we come in?" Harshaw asked politely. He had every intention of doing so whatever the answer. It was merely a question of tactics.

"I'm glad you've come," she said.

Thus encouraged, the two officers stepped inside and were shown into the front lounge.

"I'm sure you must be able to throw some light on Mr Palfrey's death," Harshaw said, giving her a friendly smile. "After all, you'd worked for him for a great many years, and who knows a man better than his secretary?"

"I don't wish to speak out of turn," Miss Seeberg said, showing every intention of doing so, "but I'm afraid that things had not been at all happy in the office since Mr Ritchie's departure. Mr Chance made things very difficult for Mr Palfrey."

"Do you believe that has some bearing on Mr Palfrey's death?"

She nodded. "I'm certain that Mr Chance was determined to oust Mr Palfrey from the firm."

"But surely Mr Palfrey was the senior

partner and had the lion's share of the profits."

"That didn't prevent Mr Chance scheming to get rid of him."

"In what way?"

"By fair means or foul," Miss Seeberg retorted dramatically.

"By driving him to suicide, do you mean?" Harshaw asked a trifle incredulously.

"Mr Palfrey would never have committed suicide."

"So you think he was murdered?"

"Yes."

"By Mr Chance?" Harshaw enquired with a further note of incredulity.

"There is such a thing as a contract killing," Miss Seeberg said darkly. "It's my belief he was lured to his death."

Harshaw nodded thoughtfully. Though it had not occurred to him, it was a viable theory.

"Was Mr Palfrey aware of Mr Chance's animosity towards him?" he asked.

"He was aware of it, but chose to regard it with scorn. Mr Palfrey wasn't easily frightened. In fact, I've never known him afraid of anything or anyone."

"It's been suggested to me that he'd recently had a lot of worries on his mind, had you noticed that?"

"He was worried about this case that was in court today, but they were no more than the worries of a conscientious solicitor. Miss Ritchie was his godchild and he was upset that she had got herself into trouble. He'd always been a friend of the Ritchies and was concerned for Mr Ritchie's health."

"How did Mr and Mrs Palfrey get on?" Harshaw asked after a reflective pause.

"He was completely devoted to his wife and children. As you probably know his wife gave birth to a son last year and he was delighted about that. It meant that the baronetcy wouldn't die with his own death." She let out a heavy sigh. "And now that small boy will inherit the title when Sir Clement dies, which could be at any moment. Her eyes misted over. "Sir Crispin Palfrey," she murmured.

After a pause, Harshaw said, "Can you think of anyone who held a serious grievance against Mr Palfrey?"

"There's a man who used to be their gardener called Thorn. But if he'd wanted to kill Mr Palfrey he'd have done it more crudely. Hit him over the head with a crowbar. Something of that sort.

"Any clients with whom he was conducting a vendetta?"

Miss Seeberg pursed her lips. "Can I take it that everything I tell you is in confidence?"

"Certainly."

"I wouldn't want the office to know what I say."

"They won't from me."

"Mr Charles Scott-Pearce was extremely angry when Mr Palfrey declined to continue representing his son. He abused Mr Palfrey on the phone and threatened to report him to the Law Society for unprofessional behaviour."

"That sounds more like a motive for Mr Palfrey to murder Mr Scott-Pearce than the other way about," Harshaw observed.

"I'm not saying that Mr Scott-Pearce did murder him, only that he had a motive and would, in my view, be capable of killing someone."

"Was Mr Palfrey in any way a womaniser?"

Miss Seeberg flushed. "Mr Palfrey was a gentleman," she said loftily, as though that answered the question.

Harshaw, however, was not to be put off as easily as that.

"Did he, as far as you know, have any extra-marital affairs?" he went on.

"No," she said firmly, and closed her mouth tightly to indicate that he need not expect any further help on that line of questioning.

Harshaw wondered whether Malcolm Palfrey had ever dallied with his secretary. It was difficult to envisage, but he knew that nothing was impossible.

Suddenly the telephone rang and Miss Seeberg retreated into a corner of the lounge to answer it.

"I'm perfectly all right, thank you, Mr Chance," she said with chilly politeness. "Of course, I'll be in tomorrow, I'll have a lot to do . . . As a matter of fact, Chief Inspector Harshaw is here now . . . Yes, at my bungalow . . . I'm giving him what help I can . . . I'll see you in the morning, Mr Chance."

A few minutes later, Harshaw and WPC Perkins took their leave. Though nothing startling had emerged from the interview, Harshaw was left wondering why Adrian Chance hadn't wanted them to see her. Suddenly a thought occurred to him: was it because he wished to go through his late partner's desk before Miss Seeberg could do so? Was that the reason he had sent her home? It was a possibility to be borne in mind.

"Let's get along to the hospital," he said when they were back in the car. "Dr Rudd should have completed the PM by now."

★ ★ ★

Harshaw found Dr Rudd sitting in a corner of the mortuary talking to a young man who had reddish hair and a rather jolly face. They each had a mug of coffee and were wearing surgical gowns.

"This is Dr Dansfield," Rudd said, introducing his companion. "He's come along to see how it's done."

Harshaw and Dansfield exchanged greetings. Pathology must be one of the courses on offer from the Youth Training Scheme, Harshaw reflected as he gazed at Dr Rudd's assistant, who looked even younger at close quarters.

In the centre of the mortuary lay Malcolm Palfrey on a sort of catafalque. A white plastic sheet covered his body from feet to shoulders, leaving only his head exposed to view. As a result of the pathologist's ministrations this was now an even less attractive sight than it had been at the scene of his death. Harshaw was glad that WPC Perkins had remained outside. He had given her the option of coming in with him, but she had said that unless it was an order, she wasn't volunteering. She had been in a mortuary once previously and it had made her feel sick. In a curious way, this made Harshaw think more highly of her.

The three men stood staring down at the unsightly head that had once been the vital component of a human being.

Rudd, who had put back on a pair of surgical gloves, pointed at the dead man's right cheek.

"The bullet entered just below the cheek bone and passed through the roof of the mouth, smashing a few teeth on its way, on through the frontal lobe of the brain until it struck the parietal bone at the top of his head at the rear. It fractured the bone, but didn't penetrate it."

"Do you have what's left of the bullet?"

Rudd picked up a small plastic envelope which was lodged between the dead man's ankles and which contained a distorted piece of metal.

"Here it is, though I'm not sure that it tells you very much."

Harshaw gave the pathologist a quizzical look. "So was it suicide or murder?"

Rudd sighed. "I've been discussing that with David Dansfield. One can't absolutely exclude suicide, though we incline to think it wasn't a self-inflicted wound. There are faint scorch marks around the entry wound which means he could have fired the pistol himself. As against that your normal suicide holds the weapon against his temple and the bullet passes clean through the head and exits on the opposite side. Someone intent on suicide doesn't usually shoot himself through the cheek because it makes death less certain. All he may do

111

is make a mess of his face. Of course it's not unknown for a suicide to place the muzzle of the weapon in his mouth and blow off the back of his head, but this fellow didn't adopt either of what I might call the established methods. Moreover, he didn't even hold the pistol up against his cheek or the scorch marks would have been much more obvious."

Harshaw was thoughtful for a while. "I was hoping you'd be able to exclude either suicide or murder, whichever."

"I wish I could oblige, though it still remains my view that the wound was not self-inflicted. That means you're looking for a murderer."

"Is that what you'll say to the coroner?"

"It's what I'll tell anyone who wants to hear." He gave Harshaw a quick sidelong look. "Come on, cheer up, I'm sure you must have someone in your sights who looks like a murderer."

"That's the problem, I haven't. Suspicion has been cast in various directions, but there's nobody I can go out and grab by the collar. I shall have to turn over a lot more stones yet before I get any worthwhile leads."

"It was a funny place for a solicitor to go and meet someone on a winter's night," Rudd said in a reflective tone. Doesn't that provide some sort of lead?"

Harshaw gave a morose shake of the head. "If he had a mistress, he'd hardly have selected Pan's Place as a rendezvous."

"Perhaps the person he went to meet chose it," Dr Dansfield remarked.

"Well, I wish you luck," Rudd said, peeling off his gloves and preparing to leave. "You know how to get in touch with me if you need. I'll let the coroner have my report as soon as may be. In fact, I'd probably better phone him and tell him my findings." He gave Harshaw a smile. "Pocket tape recorders have revolutionised our work," he said. "Now we can chop and saw and talk into the handy little machine all at the same time."

Harshaw smiled back, but his thoughts were elsewhere.

"The inquest is bound to be adjourned for police enquiries once the coroner has heard formal evidence of death and identification. Would you be prepared to attend and say why you think it's murder?"

"Certainly, if that'll help anyone."

"It might make the murderer nervous," Harshaw said with a note of hope. "And nervous people make mistakes and mistakes often lead guilty folk to be convicted of their crimes."

9

ROSA felt that she must keep in touch with events at Nettleford, though she wished to do so as unobtrusively as possible, which restricted the approaches she could discreetly make.

She ruled out. Adrian Chance as a source of information as she had found him an unsympathetic character. That meant she couldn't very easily ring Miss Seeberg and she certainly didn't know Nadine Palfrey well enough to phone her for a friendly chat. And as for the police, they'd want to know what her interest was. It would be insufficient to say that she and the deceased were about to co-defend in a case for that might alert the investigating officer in the very way she wished to avoid. In the end she decided that Douglas Perrick, the clerk of the court, would be her best point of contact. She had found him a congenial person and he was certain to know what was going on.

She decided to phone him after court hours that afternoon, which was the day following her abortive visit to Nettleford.

So far as Jeremy Scott-Pearce was concerned, she had heard nothing from him since they parted company the previous day. Though there was no specific reason why he should have been in touch with her, she had somehow expected to hear from him. She was also surprised that Jeremy's father had not called her to explain his absence and to enquire what was likely to happen next so far as the charge against his son was concerned.

As she waited to make her call to the clerk, she reflected ruefully on her involvement in Malcolm Palfrey's death. It was an embarrassment to say the least and placed her in a dilemma she would prefer to have avoided.

Her partner, Robin, had advised her to lie low and not get in touch with anyone.

"They'll come to you quickly enough if they feel it necessary," he had remarked. "And by 'they', I mean the police."

It was sound advice, but not what

Rosa wanted to hear. She felt she must find out what had happened in the past twenty-four hours.

"It's Rosa Epton, Mr Perrick," she said when she got through to him that afternoon. "I apologise for troubling you, but I'm keen to know how the police investigation is going. I didn't want to bother them, but I thought you'd probably be in touch with events."

"There's not very much to tell, save that it looks like murder rather than suicide. That's on the evidence of the pathologist. I understand the coroner will open an inquest the day after tomorrow and then adjourn it pending police enquiries."

"Who is the coroner?"

"George Shubert. He's been our coroner for donkey's years and his father held the appointment before him. He's a benign old boy and gets on with everyone. He's especially good at extending sympathy to the bereaved, which is a useful attribute seeing that most of his work arises out of fatal road accidents." After a pause, he went on, "Are you thinking of attending the inquest?"

"Yes, but I wouldn't want anyone to misinterpret my presence."

"In what way?"

"That I'm showing undue interest in something that doesn't strictly concern me."

"I'd have thought you had a perfectly legitimate interest. I can't see why there should be any raised eyebrows."

"I'm glad you think that," Rosa remarked. "After all, I shan't be attending in any official capacity."

"Maybe not, but you obviously have a personal interest in developments. At this stage nobody knows where the lightning will strike, but that doesn't mean one shouldn't keep a weather eye open."

"That's how I see it, too," Rosa said in a relieved tone. "Incidentally, is anyone under suspicion for the murder?"

"I haven't heard any names mentioned. I imagine Harshaw and his boys are in the process of interviewing anyone who might have information. I know they've spent most of today focusing their attention on Palfrey's office. Presumably they're hoping to find a lead as to whom he went to meet that evening. I must say it seems an extraordinary place to have chosen for a rendezvous. I can't believe it was his choice."

"Then it must have been his murderer's."

"I gather the police are interested in the movements that evening of a man named Thorn. He was the Palfreys' gardener until he got the sack a few weeks ago. He has a record for violence *and* he once worked over at Shilman Green when they needed additional help in the park. But he got the sack from there too. A hard worker from all accounts, but with a vile temper when he's crossed. Anyway he's clearly someone the police have to interview, if only to eliminate him from their enquiry. He certainly wouldn't be my number one suspect."

"Who fits that bill?"

"I think I'd prefer to keep that to myself Miss Epton," he said with a quick laugh. After a pause he added, "Drop in and say hello next time you're in Nettleford."

"Thanks. I will. And thank you for your help."

"I wasn't aware I'd given you any.

Don't make me nervous!"

Rosa laughed and rang off

★ ★ ★

Two days later Rosa set off in her car for Nettleford once more. The inquest was timed for twelve o'clock and she decided to call at Shilman Green on her way. She wanted to see the scene of Malcolm Palfrey's death for herself, motivated more by curiosity than by any conviction that she was serving her client's interest.

Leaving the car in the station yard, she walked round the corner and entered the park. She spotted Pan's Place immediately. Rejecting the direct approach across wet grass, she kept to the asphalted path for as long as she could. She didn't wish to arrive at the coroner's court looking as though she had been on a cross-country run. On reaching the crescent of bushes that screened Pan's Place from the rest of the park, she felt a small quiver of excitement. Entering the enclosed area she gazed at Pan on his stone plinth in the centre and at the three wooden seats spaced around him. So this was where Malcolm Palfrey met his end! She was just reflecting on this when a voice startled her.

"Can I help you?"

She swung round, blushing as if she had just been caught shop-lifting. A young man in a dark blue donkey jacket and holding a long rake was staring at her.

"No, it's all right, thank you," she stammered. "I was just looking. I'm not trespassing, am I?"

"Not as far as I'm concerned," he said, observing her with a steady look. "Are you connected with the police investigation?"

"No. I'm a solicitor. It just happens that I was due to co-defend in a case with Mr Palfrey the day he was found dead."

"I was the person who discovered the body. My name's Tom Berry. What's yours?"

"Rosa Epton."

"You're not local, are you?"

"No, from London."

"I used to live in London," he remarked, passing the rake from one hand to the other. "I'm glad to be out of it."

"Were you a park-keeper there?"

He shook his head. "A medical student, but I chucked it in. Or rather it chucked me in. I had a bit of a breakdown and my doctor advised me to go to the country and take an outdoor job. He reckoned it would be the best therapy and, surprisingly, he was right."

All the while he spoke, his eyes never left Rosa's face. There was something compelling about his gaze, though nothing remarkable about the rest of him. He was average height with medium brown hair and a small tip-tilted nose. There was faint stubble on his upper lip and at the sides of his chin which indicated he had not shaved that morning. He had a well-formed mouth which, to her shock and horror, Rosa suddenly felt she would like to kiss. She shook her head briskly as if to dissolve this obtrusive thought.

"I'd better get back to my car," she said a trifle hoarsely.

"Anything you'd like to know?" he

enquired. "I've told the police everything, but that doesn't mean I can't talk to you as well."

"I can't think of anything at the moment. Maybe later . . . "

"I'll look forward to that," he said, smiling for the first time. It was a nice smile and caused Rosa's heart to flutter. "I may have had a nervous breakdown but I'm not your retarded village yokel."

"I'd have said you were anything but retarded," observed Rosa as she turned and left the scene, determined not to look back as she made her way across the park.

Her mind was in a turmoil, for she knew her chemistry well enough to realise that her encounter with Tom Berry had combustible possibilities. There had always been a type of young man whose appearance alone could ignite her emotions. Robin Snaith regarded it as her Achilles heel and was apt to worry about the consequences, though so far she had always managed to survive relatively unscathed those emotional adventures she had experienced.

She didn't know how old Tom Berry

was, save that he was obviously younger than herself.

For heaven's sake, Rosa, she murmured, half in alarm, half in tingling hope, you'll be snatching them from their cradles next. Don't be silly, another voice broke in, he's been a medical student and is far from being an innocent. Anyway, the odds are you'll never see him again.

* * *

The coroner's court was a Victorian barnlike structure with a high vaulted ceiling and rows of wooden seats worn smooth over the years.

There were fewer than a dozen people when Rosa arrived. The coroner hadn't yet taken his seat and the atmosphere was one of quiet somnolence.

Two reporters were talking earnestly to someone whom Rosa later learnt was Detective Inspector Harshaw. Sitting alone in the lawyer's row was a counsel whose face was familiar but whose name escaped her. She wondered on whose behalf he was appearing.

Not being there in any official capacity,

she went and sat in the seats reserved for the public, where a number of old men were taking refuge from the cold outside. Courts always attracted a number of devotees who followed the proceedings with the intensity of punters at a race meeting. Avoiding these connoisseurs of the forensic scene, Rosa took a seat in an empty row at the back.

She was suddenly aware that Adrian Chance had arrived in court and was talking to the barrister in counsel's row. She deduced that he must be holding a watching brief on behalf of Palfrey and Co., which seemed unnecessary at this stage. Presumably, however, Malcolm Palfrey's surviving partner intended to have an eye kept on everything that happened in court.

Silence was called for and the coroner entered and took his seat. He wished everyone good morning and Rosa was reminded of a Santa Claus without beard and whiskers.

"This is an inquisition into the death of Malcolm Palfrey on 2nd December last. I now call Detective Chief Inspector Harshaw."

Harshaw stepped into the witness box and took the oath. In answer to the coroner's questions, he said that he was the officer in charge of enquiries into Mr Palfrey's death and went on to describe where the body was found and by whom.

Mr Shubert nodded keenly and Rosa almost expected him to call for a round of applause.

Harshaw went on to give a few further details concerning identification and the like and then stopped, giving the coroner a meaningful look.

"I take it, Chief Inspector, that you would like me to adjourn my inquisition so that you may continue your enquiries? Before I do so, however, I think it might be helpful if I called Dr Rudd who performed the post mortem examination and who has supplied me with one of his always helpful reports."

The pathologist, who was hovering close to the witness box, received the accolade with a small nod and stepped forward to give his evidence.

The coroner led him carefully through his report so that Dr Rudd's evidence consisted of a series of acquiescing monosyllables.

"As I understand your evidence, you formed the view that Mr Palfrey's injuries were not self-inflicted?"

"That is correct, sir."

"Though with your customary fairness, you don't absolutely exclude the possibility of suicide?"

"No."

"But you think it unlikely?"

"Yes."

For a while coroner and pathologist continued to pat the ball to and fro between them until Mr Shubert reached his final question.

"So what your evidence amounts to, Dr Rudd, is that you believe Mr Palfrey died at the hands of another person?"

"Yes."

"In circumstances that indicate homicide?"

"Yes."

"Murder or manslaughter?"

"Yes."

"Thank you, Dr Rudd, for your most helpful contribution to the court's proceedings." Turning to Harshaw, Mr

Shubert went on, "I think that's as far as I can take my inquisition today and I propose to adjourn *sine die*. Whether or not it will be necessary to re-convene the court will depend on the outcome of your enquiries, Chief Inspector.

He rose, and bestowing smiles all round, left the court.

Rosa observed Adrian Chance departing deep in conversation with his counsel. He never glanced in her direction, for which she was grateful. Harshaw, meanwhile, had become a focus of attention by the press who clearly felt there was a story in the offing. Rosa who had been wondering whether to introduce herself to him now decided against and slipped out unnoticed. She would return to London and watch developments from there.

It was two days later that Jeremy Scott-Pearce phoned and said in an anxious voice that the police wished to interview him at Nettleford and what was he to do?

"I'll call them and find out what it's all about," Rosa said in a calming tone.

When she got through to the police, a somewhat tight-lipped sergeant told her that Chief Inspector Harshaw wished to interview her client as a matter of routine.

"I could arrange for you to see him here at my office," Rosa said.

"It'll be more convenient at the station, Miss Epton," the officer replied.

Convenient for whom, Rosa felt like asking. It seemed best, however, to play along with police wishes for the present. Accordingly, an appointment was made for the next day.

Rosa believed she knew why the police were insistent on the interview taking place on their own ground, but she didn't wish to alarm Jeremy by telling him. She was long aware that clients took small comfort in being told they had nothing to fear if they were innocent. Apart from anything else, it was often not true.

Clearly the investigation had progressed in the past two days. She wished she knew in what direction. Who else, she wondered, was being interviewed 'as a matter of routine'?

10

ON this occasion Jeremy consented to accompany Rosa in her car. They met at Snaith and Epton's office at ten-thirty and set off immediately.

"You ought to have a BMW," he said, as he got into the car.

"I prefer my small Honda. It's much easier for getting about town in and certainly far easier to park."

"I suppose so," he murmured. "But wouldn't you like something a bit zippier for a long journey?"

"If I have to make a long journey, I borrow a BMW from one of my friends," Rosa remarked.

He fell silent for several minutes and when he spoke again, his tone was both aggrieved and truculent. "What on earth do the police want to interview *me* for? I can't tell them anything."

"I imagine they're interviewing everyone who was in recent touch with Mr Palfrey."

"They can't believe that I murdered him."

"I'm sure they don't."

"What motive could I possibly have had?"

"You tell me."

"I didn't have one either to murder him or anyone else for that matter. I'd be incapable of killing somebody in cold blood." He stared morosely out of the window for a while. "Nadine believes that Adrian Chance is in something up to his neck."

"When did you speak to Nadine Palfrey?"

"We had a long chat on the phone two nights ago. She says that Malcolm didn't trust his partner and wanted to have a special audit of the firm's accounts, but refrained because of the rumpus it would cause."

"Has she told the police that?"

"She's waiting for the right moment to do so." He gave Rosa a sly glance. "Did you know Miss Seeberg used to be a member of a revolver club?"

Rosa shook her head. "Is that something else Mrs Palfrey told you?"

"Actually, I knew, but had forgotten."

"Are you suggesting that makes her a suspect?"

"I'm not pointing fingers at anyone," he said, with a shrug.

"It'd be as well to stick to that when we meet the police. Incidentally, they're bound to ask you to account for your movements on the evening Mr Palfrey met his death. What'll you tell them?"

"I usually go to a keep fit class at a nearby gym on Wednesday, but what with the case coming up the next day, I was feeling edgy and couldn't face an evening of strenuous exercise, so I stayed in and watched television. The only time I went out was to fetch a Chinese takeaway from a place in the King's Road." He grimaced in recollection. "It was obviously their sweet and sour prawns that made me ill."

"Was your mother at home?"

"No, she goes to a bridge club most evenings."

"The police will want to know if there's anyone who can corroborate your movements?"

He gave a gloomy shake of his head.

"I was alone in the flat, except when I went to the takeaway and nobody there would be likely to remember me. I don't stand out like a sore thumb in the King's Road, I'm just part of the scene. Anyway, why should I try and polish an alibi?"

"I was merely anticipating what the police are likely to ask you."

"Yes, OK, I'm sorry, I didn't mean to sound so touchy."

"It's important that you remain calm and polite when we're at the police station. Don't try and score cheap points, the police don't like that."

He gave her a rueful smile. "Yes, ma'am, I'll remember."

On arrival at Nettleford, Rosa parked in the market place from where it was a mere one hundred and fifty yards' walk to the police station. The officer on duty at the front desk looked up with interest when Rosa announced their identities.

"If you'll just hang on," he said, "I'll let Detective Chief Inspector Harshaw know you're here."

Five minutes later a glass-panelled

swing door was pushed open and a man smoking a small evil-smelling cigar appeared.

"You Jeremy Scott-Pearce?" he said.

"Yes."

"And I'm his solicitor," Rosa said in a steely tone.

"I'm Detective Sergeant Whitehead," he said, eyeing Rosa with disfavour. "Follow me and I'll take you up to the Chief Inspector."

Harshaw rose as they entered his office and waved at two hard-back chairs. "Do sit down. I'm afraid there's not much room, but at least we can have a chair apiece." Turning to Rosa, he went on, "I believe I saw you at the coroners court the other day?"

"Yes. I was there out of curiosity."

Harshaw gave a small nod, but made no comment. To Jeremy, he said, "Now, Mr Scott-Pearce, I'd be glad if you'd tell me your movements on the Wednesday evening in question, say between eight and eleven o'clock."

Jeremy repeated in a nervous voice what he had told Rosa on their way to Nettleford. From time to time his eyes strayed anxiously to the tape recorder on Harshaw's desk.

"You didn't come to Nettleford that evening?" Harshaw enquired.

"No."

"Did you speak to Mr Palfrey that day?"

"No, I didn't have any cause to, as he wasn't representing me any longer."

"I gather he felt a conflict of interest had arisen as between yourself and Miss Ritchie."

"That's what he said."

"Perhaps I can explain," Rosa broke in.

"Thank you, Miss Epton," Harshaw said when she had finished. Turning back to Jeremy he went on, "I imagine you weren't very pleased with Mr Palfrey for throwing you overboard?"

Jeremy shrugged. "There wasn't much I could do about it."

"Did you have an argument?"

"No, but my father . . . " He let the sentence trail away and closed his mouth.

"What were you about to say concerning your father?"

"He was annoyed and phoned Mr Palfrey to say so."

"That all?"

"Yes."

"Did you ever threaten Mr Palfrey for what he'd done?"

"Definitely not."

"Did you remain on good terms?"

"Yes."

"How long had you known him?"

"Virtually all my life."

"Knowing him as well as you did, can you give me any help as to who might have killed him?"

Jeremy shook his head. "I'm afraid not. He belonged to my parents generation and I knew nothing about his life or his business affairs."

"I believe you were friendly with his wife?"

Jeremy glared. "She's always been very kind to me," he said stiffly.

"Might her husband have been jealous of your friendship with his wife?"

"If you think Nadine and I had an affair, you're quite wrong. She's far too wrapped up in her family to want to flirt."

Stop there, Rosa thought. You've said enough on the subject.

"Would you like to have flirted with her?" Harshaw enquired mildly.

"I've never given it any thought. On the whole I prefer girls of my own age."

"What do you mean by 'on the whole'?"

"I prefer girls of my own age, stop, Jeremy said with a touch of annoyance.

"Well, I think that's about all for the moment, Mr Scott-Pearce, though there is just one further thing. Purely as a matter of routine, we'd like to have a sample of your blood and of your head hair. And I'm sure you won't mind giving us your fingerprints at the same time."

Jeremy turned toward Rosa with an anxious expression,while she fixed Harshaw with a firm look.

"Can you assure me that this really is a matter of routine, Chief Inspector?"

"Yes."

"And that my client's fingerprints will be destroyed as soon as the case is over?"

"That's normal procedure, as you know,

Miss Epton, always provided they're not on record in respect of previous criminal activity."

"I'd have thought you would already have checked that Mr Scott-Pearce doesn't have a criminal record."

"I have," Harshaw replied equably, "and he's not on the computer under that name."

"Or any other name," Jeremy broke in indignantly.

"Then you have nothing to worry about, sir," Harshaw observed. "Now, if you'd go with Sergeant Whitehead . . . it won't take more than a few minutes." He glanced at Rosa. "I'm assuming, Miss Epton, that you're not going to advise your client against co-operating with us?"

Rosa could see that Jeremy was reluctant to accompany Sergeant Whitehead who had got up and was standing by the door with an air of impatience. She knew, however, that it would be tactically foolish to refuse co-operation and gestured him to go.

"How's your investigation going?" she asked when she and Chief Inspector

Harshaw were alone.

"It's a case with a number of very odd features," he said with a sigh. "The so-far unanswered question is, what took Mr Palfrey to Pan's Place on a dark winter's night?"

"Armed, too."

"Exactly."

"Are you satisfied that he was killed by his own gun?"

"I've not yet had the result of lab tests, but everything points to that. The weapon found on the ground beside him had definitely been fired. If he didn't commit suicide, he obviously went out armed, expecting trouble. What trouble, I'd like to know?"

"Were there fingerprints on the weapon?"

"Yes, his."

"Doesn't that indicate suicide?"

Harshaw gave a helpless shrug. "Maybe that'll be the final conclusion."

"I imagine what you're looking for is someone with a motive.

"Ah! Find me such a person, Miss Epton, and I can go to work." He sighed. "Motive is like the trail of paper in a paperchase. You and I both know that motive isn't an ingredient of murder, but try telling that to a jury! And I don't blame them." He paused and plucked at his lower lip. "The only person with a smidgeon of a motive is a disgruntled ex-employee of Mr Palfrey's. A gardener who got the sack and was later heard to issue threats against Mr Palfrey. We're checking his alibi, but somehow he just doesn't fit the picture of a murderer in this case. Even if I got a confession out of him, I'd want to double-check it.

"There are subtleties about Mr Palfrey's death and there's nothing subtle about Phil Thorn." There was silence for a while, then Harshaw said suddenly, "What was your impression of Mr Palfrey?"

"It was better to be on his side than against him," Rosa said after a moment's thought. "He was always very pleasant to me, but I didn't know him at all well. I'd met him only once before this present case and that was two years ago."

"Were you surprised when he approached you about young Scott-Pearce's defence?"

"Yes."

"It came out of the blue?"

"Yes." After a pause she said, "I trust you don't think our case had any bearing on his death?"

"Do you think it might have?"

"I can't see how."

"Just a coincidence then?"

"It has to be. For me an embarrassing one."

"In what way?"

But Rosa wasn't inclined to be interrogated further.

Glancing at her watch, she said, "It's taking a long time to obtain this hair and blood sample . . . "

"There may have been a queue. Your client isn't the only person assisting our enquiries this morning." He sat back in his chair and stretched like a dog that has just woken up. "You certainly meet all sorts and conditions in our job," he went on. "Did you know that the young chap who discovered the body was an ex-medical student turned park-keeper?"

Rosa could only stare back foolishly as she fought to control her blush. She was aware that he was eyeing her with a puzzled expression, as well he might.

141

To her great relief, the door opened and Jeremy and Sergeant Whitehead returned.

"Thank God, that's over," Jeremy said as they walked back to Rosa's car. "I've had enough dealings with the police to last me the rest of my life." He made a face. "As for Sergeant Whitehead, I wouldn't trust him an inch. He'd as soon frame you as shake your hand. Did the Chief Inspector tell you anything interesting?"

"He didn't seem entirely persuaded that Mr Palfrey committed suicide."

"But does he have any murder suspects lined up?"

"I gathered not."

"It seems the police have been obtaining blood and hair samples from all and sundry, even from Nadine and the Italian au pair."

"That would be for purposes of elimination."

"I was relieved to find out that I wasn't the only one."

"You didn't really believe that you'd been singled out, did you?"

"I don't know what I believed. I'm

just glad it's over — for the time being at least." He sounded quite cheerful.

Rosa gave him a sidelong glance. He was clearly a person of rapidly changing moods.

"I'm afraid the criminal damage case is likely to be hanging over you for some time," she remarked, as she manoeuvred the car out of the market place.

His expression clouded over. "I'd almost forgotten about that."

11

MISS SEEBERG and her sister phoned each other regularly every Sunday. They took it in turns to initiate the call, but thereafter the pattern was the same, Madge Seeberg did most of the talking and her sister, Dolly, most of the listening. Dolly, who was a widow, lived in a village in Lincolnshire with three cats and a parrot named Joseph.

On the second Sunday after Malcolm Palfrey's death, it was Miss Seeberg's turn to make the call and she did so at the moment she reckoned her sister would be back from church.

"I don't know how much longer I can stand this, Doll," she said as soon as her sister had lifted the receiver and the usual enquiries about each other's health were over.

"The atmosphere in the office is so strained, it's beginning to affect my nerves. Of course, I never expected it to be the same without Mr Palfrey, but Mr Chance is really showing himself in his true colours. As you know, he and Mr Palfrey never did get on and now he's almost dancing on his grave, except that poor Mr Palfrey hasn't yet been buried. It's disgusting the way they leave a body in the mortuary refrigerator until the coroner issues a death certificate. I've known it take weeks, even months, in some cases. Anyway, I have no intention of staying on. I shall leave as soon as I can — Did you say something, dear?"

"Has anyone been arrested yet?"

"No and that's another thing. If you ask me, the police needn't look very far afield to find their man."

"You really do think it's — "

"Mr C? Yes, I do, I happen to know he's in financial difficulties. He has a huge mortgage on his house and his wife gets through money as if it grew on trees all the year round."

"Do you think you should say things like that, Madge?"

"It's the truth. Just wait until the Law

Society's accountant starts turning over a few stones. He'll find more than the odd earwig."

"How are you so sure?"

"The senior partner's personal secretary knows everything that goes on," Miss Seeberg said emphatically.

"And you really believe that Mr C killed Mr P?" her sister said with a quiver of excitement.

"I'm sure of it. He was frightened of exposure and disgrace. He could have finished up being struck off and even sent to prison."

"Do be careful, Madge," her sister said anxiously.

"Don't worry. I know how to look after myself."

"You may think so, dear, but desperate men are often driven to desperate measures. Don't underestimate the enemy, as my Fred used to say."

Madge Seeberg had never had much time for her brother-in-law, whom she regarded as a bigot with old testament views of right and wrong. On more than one occasion he had told Madge that adultery in the mind was as grave a sin as when committed between the sheets and this had not endeared him to his sister-in-law who may have been guilty of the one, but not, to her chagrin, of the other. When he died suddenly at the age of fifty-four, she had felt that it served him right, though she didn't go so far as to say so to her sister. Nevertheless, it was a fact that his death had brought the two women closer together.

"Don't do anything foolhardy, Madge," Dolly now added.

"Of course, I shan't. When you've worked for a solicitor in criminal practice for ten years, you know all the pitfalls and how to avoid them."

"Thank goodness you're a strong person. Father always used to say that you were lion-hearted and that I was afraid to say boo to a goose."

"Father was over-fond of creating silly myths," Madge Seeberg remarked tartly. After a pause, she went on, "I may call you in the course of the week, Doll, depending on developments. Meanwhile, you can give my love to the cats."

"What about Joseph?"

"I've not forgotten that he pecked my finger the last time I saw him. He doesn't deserve my love."

Dolly gave a small laugh. Nobody pecked Madge with impunity. Nevertheless, she couldn't help worrying.

Worrying and wondering.

* * *

Malcolm Palfrey had been teaching Teresa how to play bridge. She had always enjoyed card games and had relished the intellectual superiority of bridge over those she had previously played with her sister and friends. Nadine, however, didn't play bridge and so the lessons had lapsed.

On this particular Sunday evening mother and daughters were playing knock-out whist, Cressida with enjoyment, Teresa with disdain.

"I don't want to play any more," Teresa announced sulkily, after losing the first hand.

"We've only just begun," Cressida retorted indignantly.

"It's such a stupid game."

"You're only saying that because you lost."

"No, I'm not."

"You can't even win when you cheat."

"I did not cheat," Teresa replied with hauteur.

"Yes, you did. I saw you."

Before Nadine could intervene and pour oil on the troubled waters, Teresa had got up and was flouncing out of the room.

"You shouldn't have accused her of cheating," she said to her younger daughter.

"But she did cheat, Mummy."

"I'm sure she didn't mean to."

Cressida gave her mother a pitying look and began to gather up the cards.

"You can't cheat without meaning to."

"She's not herself. She's missing Daddy very much."

"I just hope that Crispin doesn't grow up like her," Cressida remarked darkly.

Nadine looked at her daughter with a puzzled frown.

"What do you mean?"

"He and Teresa were both born in

Italy. I'm the only one who was born in England."

Nadine smiled indulgently. "Because they were born in Italy doesn't give them similar temperaments."

"There's a girl in my class and she says that where you're born affects the way you think. Her name's Harriet Tidmarsh."

"Where was she born?" Nadine enquired amiably.

"In Japan."

"How has that affected her?"

"She's like an electric eel. She was born prematurely because of an earthquake and she says she can foretell disasters."

"I can see that the earthquake might have had an unconscious effect on her," Nadine said carefully, "but not the fact she was born in Japan. Anyway, you and Teresa don't have different characters because you happened to be born in different countries. That's an absurd notion. You get your genes from your parents, not from the environment."

Cressida looked thoughtful. "I still wouldn't want Crispin to have been born near Vesuvius when it was erupting."

"Then you can stop worrying because

150

he wasn't." After a pause, Nadine went on, "Why don't you go and find Teresa and ask her to come back?"

Cressida got up, but her mind was clearly elsewhere.

"I wonder what Daddy's doing now?" she said in a reflective tone. "Do you think he's watching us?"

"Would you like that?"

"I'm not sure."

The door opened and Teresa reappeared.

"Are you still playing?"

"We were waiting in the hope that you'd come back," her mother replied.

"Do you think Daddy can see us?" Cressida asked her sister.

Teresa put on a ferocious frown as tears welled up in her eyes. Then turning she dashed from the room.

"She really is being very emotional," Cressida observed dispassionately.

Nadine sighed as she prepared to go after her elder daughter. Malcolm had always had a particular soft spot for their first-born, though he endeavoured not to show any undue favouritism. Cressida's birth had been overshadowed by his disappointment that she wasn't a boy. He had been quite certain she would be the son he wanted.

As she went upstairs, Nadine reflected on the problems that lay ahead. It was not going to be easy to re-shape her life. There were so many imponderables surrounding Malcolm's death, as well as secrets she dare not share with anyone.

★ ★ ★

"Is that you, Adrian?" Clare Chance called out when she heard the front door open.

"Yes. Sorry, I'm late."

"Late! I thought you must have decided not to come back for lunch. I've had mine. Yours is in the oven, but I don't guarantee it'll still be edible." Her husband appeared in the living-room doorway and she went on, "Where've you been all this time?"

"At the office."

"What on earth have you been doing there on a Sunday morning?"

"There's a lot of work in connection with Malcolm Palfrey's death."

"Were you there alone?"

"Entirely alone," he said with a small wintry smile.

"Wouldn't a secretary have been of help?"

"I preferred to be on my own."

"His death isn't going to cause difficulties, is it?"

"I hope not."

"What I meant was, you won't have any trouble taking over his share of the partnership?"

"That'll be a matter for negotiation with Nadine. The bulk of his estate is left to her on trust. Amanda Ritchie and one or two others receive small legacies, but that's all."

"I can't think why he didn't make you an executor."

"It doesn't worry me."

"Well, at least we'll have a bit more money now he's dead."

"Eventually."

"Why do these things take so long?"

"Because it's always been so. In any event, we've yet to see where the police investigation leads."

Clare Chance gave a disdainful shrug.

"I wonder if they've been in touch with Charles Scott-Pearce. It would be interesting to know why he didn't turn up at court when his son was due to appear. You told me that he was expected, but never came."

"For all I know, the police have been in touch with him."

"I never liked that man. And as for the way he walked out on his wife . . . He could be quite ruthless."

"Well, there's no suggestion that he killed Palfrey."

"That doesn't mean he didn't."

Adrian Chance shrugged. "I'd better go and rescue my lunch from the oven."

"You'd probably do better to make yourself a sandwich."

"There's some ham in the fridge."

As he retreated to the kitchen, he reflected on the mess he was in. Fending off creditors was almost a full-time job. Moreover, not one in which his wife offered any assistance.

There had been a time when he wondered if she and Malcolm Palfrey were having an affair. But there had never been any evidence as such. Perhaps the fact that they were very alike in character made it improbable.

★ ★ ★

Charles Scott-Pearce felt guilty at having deserted his son on the day of his trial, but once he knew of Malcolm Palfrey's death, he realised that the case wouldn't go ahead and that his best course was to remove himself.

He had known Palfrey for over twenty years and had respected him as an astute and hard-headed lawyer. The solicitor had acted for him in a variety of matters and they had also been partners in a number of deals, some of which had brought them close to the fine line that divides what is legal from what is on the wrong side of the law. Scott-Pearce had always had an entrepreneurial eye open for making a fast buck and Palfrey had been a useful ally.

Though never close friends, their long-standing association had seemed to be firmly based. That was why he had been furious when the solicitor announced that he could no longer defend Jeremy in court. He had told Palfrey in no uncertain terms what he thought of him.

Now, however, his main concern was that Palfrey hadn't left any incriminating documents behind that might fall into the wrong hands. He found it deeply frustrating to be on the sidelines and unable to influence events. And not only frustrating, but potentially perilous.

It might be better to fly over to London where he could keep in closer touch with developments. He could also keep a protective eye on his son.

He had no need to speculate about who killed Malcolm Palfrey. He knew.

★ ★ ★

Debbie Noakes felt that she was in love for the first time in her life. Seeing that she was only seventeen, this was not especially remarkable. But she was a born romantic and in her star-struck eyes Tom Berry was the perfect Prince Charming. She glorified his virtues and ignored his frailties. The first time he made love to her she had soared up on to cloud nine and had remained there ever since. This somewhat dismayed Tom who hadn't wished their relationship to turn into one of cloying attachment.

"I love you so much, Tom," she murmured as she nuzzled against his bare chest that Sunday afternoon. "I want us to be together forever."

"Let's enjoy one day at a time," he said cautiously. "We're too young to think of settling down."

"But you're twenty-five, Tom. And you're so mature."

Tom winced. "I still don't know my own mind," he said.

"But you do love me, don't you?"

"You know the answer to that," he said evasively.

She snuggled closer. "Do you know how long we've known one another?"

"About two months, isn't it?"

"It's ninety-four days today."

"Oh."

"What shall we do to celebrate our hundredth day?"

"We'll think of something."

"I know what I'd like us to do," she said, and waited for him to reply. When he remained silent, she went on, "Go and

157

stop the night in a really posh hotel."

"And end up at the police station because we couldn't pay the bill."

"But it'd be lovely if we could, wouldn't it?"

"I can think of better ways of spending a hundred pounds."

"But if we *could* afford it, you would like that, wouldn't you?"

"Yes, but we can't, so forget it. Perhaps we'll go to that new pizza place in Nettleford."

"Or up to London for the evening?"

"Perhaps."

"And afterwards come back here to your room?"

"We don't want your parents asking awkward questions."

"They think you're a good influence on me."

Tom let out a silent groan, as he wondered how he could loosen the tentacles she had fastened on him without hurting her.

"Do you remember where we went the very first time we met?" she went on, as she stroked his face.

"Yes, Pan's Place in the park."

She gave a small shiver. "I don't want to go there ever again after what's happened."

"Once spring is here, it'll be as popular with courting couples as it ever was. It takes more than a murder to put people off."

"You were so brave, Tom," she murmured. "I'd have been scared, but you might have been discovering bodies every day the calm way you behaved and sent for help."

She raised her head and looked down into his eyes before giving him a long and lingering kiss.

The trouble was that it was Rosa's face which filled his mind's eye.

12

JEREMY had just inserted the key into the door lock of his car, which was parked outside the flats where he lived, when the two men who had been watching him from the pavement closed in on either side.

"You're coming with us," Sergeant Whitehead said reaching for the key.

"Like bloody hell I am!" Jeremy exclaimed as he tried to make a dash for it. But the second man tripped him before he had gone a couple of paces, then hauled him unceremoniously to his feet.

"Resisting arrest only makes things worse," Whitehead said in a satisfied tone.

"Arrest? What the hell are you talking about?"

"This is Detective Constable Briggs. He plays rugger for the police so I advise you not to try anything funny. Our car's across the road and we're taking you to Nettleford."

"I demand to phone my solicitor," Jeremy said in a taut voice.

"There'll be plenty of time for that later on."

"My mother'll be home soon and she'll wonder where I am."

"Not to worry. We'll get a message to her."

"I want to see the warrant."

"What warrant?"

"The warrant for my arrest."

Sergeant Whitehead grinned malevolently. "We don't need a warrant. Not for murder. Anyway, you're coming along to help us in our enquiries. Now, don't let's waste any more time."

With DC Briggs holding his arm in a fierce grip, Jeremy was steered across the road to the waiting car. Shoving him roughly into the back, Whitehead got in beside him, while DC Briggs eased his muscular frame into the driver's seat.

"It'll save everyone time and trouble if we have a chat on the way," Whitehead said, as he lit a small cigar and blew a plume of smoke in Jeremy's direction. "If you take my advice, you'll come clean. We've got you bang to rights and we can make things easier for you if you cooperate. That's right, isn't it, Derek?"

"Absolutely, skipper. I'm sure Jeremy — it is Jeremy, isn't it? — will see where his best interests lie."

"Let's hope so," said Whitehead.

"I refuse to say anything until I can see my solicitor," Jeremy retorted.

"That sort of talk won't get you anywhere," Whitehead said. "If you want us to pass messages to your mother and let Ms Epton know where you are, you've got to act sensibly. It's up to you, but I can tell you that the cells at Nettleford police station aren't exactly luxurious and they can become pretty lonely places after a few hours on your tod." He gave a small unpleasant laugh. "But at least they're soundproof That's right, isn't it, Derek?"

"It certainly is. You can bellow your head off and nobody'll hear."

"You've no right to . . . to . . . detain me like this."

"Now, if there's one thing I don't appreciate, it's being told by young squirts that I don't know my rights. However, I'll overlook it if you behave sensibly for the rest of the journey. But I mean, sensibly. You killed Palfrey, didn't you?"

"You're crazy."

Jeremy let out a grunt of pain as Sergeant Whitehead's elbow caught him a vicious jab in the ribs.

"'Fraid my elbow slipped," Whitehead remarked. "Now, where were we? Yes, I remember, you were about to tell me why you shot Palfrey." Jeremy shook his head and the officer went on, "He provoked you, did he? Provocation could reduce it to manslaughter and you wouldn't get such a heavy sentence."

"You're wrong," Jeremy said in a tired voice. "I'd never kill anyone."

"You only throw lighted fireworks through innocent folks' letter-boxes, is that it?" Sergeant Whitehead said in a hectoring tone. "Anyone who can do that wouldn't think twice about committing murder. That's my view, anyway." He blew further cigar smoke into Jeremy's face, causing him to turn his head sharply away. "Don't look out of the window when I'm talking to you, it's rude. Look at me!" Jeremy turned his head slowly back again, his facial muscles as stiff as if they'd been sand-blasted. "So far you've not done yourself much good, but you still have time to show a bit of sense. We know you killed Palfrey, so admit it and make things easier for yourself. If you don't help yourself, nobody else will."

"You've no right to . . . " He let out a cry of pain as the tip of Whitehead's cigar touched the back of his hand.

"Didn't burn you, did I? No room to move in the back of this car. Now, you were about to say something, I think?"

"No."

"Yes, you were. You were about to tell me I had no right to do something or other. Go on, say it, get it off your chest." When Jeremy remained silent he went on, "Perhaps you were about to tell me I had no right to accuse you of murder. Was that it?"

"I demand to see my solicitor before I answer any more of your questions."

"Oh, it's demands now, is it?" Whitehead said unpleasantly. "Well, you listen to me, sonny, you'll see your solicitor just as soon as we decide it's convenient and not a moment before. So you can stop trying to intimidate me."

"If you take my advice, Jeremy," DC Briggs said over his shoulder, "you'll treat Sergeant Whitehead as decently as he's treating you. He doesn't like being threatened with solicitors. He can help you if you let him."

"You heard what DC Briggs said, so now let's have a bit of sense out of you. Was it you or Palfrey who suggested meeting at Pan's Place?"

"Neither of us. We didn't have any arrangement to meet."

"One of you must have proposed it. I may look an idiot, but I'm not going to believe you met there as a result of telepathy. So let's have the truth."

"Just leave me alone."

"Self-pity isn't going to get you anywhere. I'm giving you the chance to make a clean breast of things. If you do that, I can help you. Might even be able to arrange bail."

"Bail?" Jeremy exclaimed in an alarmed voice.

"That's what I said."

"But I haven't been charged."

"That's merely a matter of time. Of course, without bail you can look forward to spending the next few months in custody. And that's only the beginning. Life imprisonment is what you get for murder. Admittedly, you'd get out before you had a long grey beard, but at your age even ten years isn't much to look forward to. So I strongly advise you to start talking now."

"Oh, my God!" Jeremy whispered and began to cry.

★ ★ ★

It was later the same morning that Stephanie buzzed Rosa and announced that someone called Tom Berry would like to speak to her on the phone.

"He says he's a park-keeper at Shilman Green," Stephanie went on in her driest tone, "and that you know him. Do you want me to put him through?"

Rosa felt her throat contract as she said as casually as she could, "Yes, I'll speak to him."

"Is that Rosa Epton?" said an immediately recognisable voice. "It's Tom Berry. Remember me?"

"I remember you very well," Rosa

said with a foolish little laugh which she wished she had stifled.

"I may be telling you what you already know, but I've just seen Jeremy Scott-Pearce being bundled out of a car and into Nettleford police station." Rosa wasn't sure what she had been expecting, but it certainly wasn't that. "I read in the local paper that you were his solicitor. I don't know if you still are," Tom went on, "so you're free to tell me to mind my own business."

"He's still my client, all right. Are you quite sure it was him you saw?"

"Yes, I had to report at the council office this morning — Shilman Green comes under Nettleford — and as I was passing the police station this car pulled up and your chap was hustled across the pavement by Sergeant Whitehead. He's one of Chief Inspector Harshaw's boys and nobody's favourite person."

Rosa's brain had been working furiously while he spoke. She was startled by the information she had received and ready, moreover, to be extremely angry at the police action.

"Thanks, Tom," she said. "I appreciate

your letting me know. I'll have to try and find out what's happening. Meanwhile, many thanks."

"I hope we'll soon be in touch again," he said. "Let me know if there's anything further I can do. Got pencil and paper handy?"

"Why?"

"I'll give you my phone number. You can get me there most evenings . . ."

"No need to give you mine," Rosa said with a small laugh, "as you obviously have it."

"I don't have your home number," he said in his seemingly guileless way.

Rosa hesitated, then heard herself say it.

During the next forty minutes she put through a number of calls to Nettleford police station. She was told variously that Detective Chief Inspector Harshaw was out; that he was speaking on another line; that he was in conference and unable to come to the phone. And no, it was impossible to say when he would be free.

Five minutes after her last call she was in her car and on her way to

Nettleford. It was only then that she fell to wondering how Tom Berry had recognised Jeremy. As far as she was aware they had never met.

★ ★ ★

Rosa parked in the market place and got out of the car, half-expecting to see Tom Berry pop out of the ground. But there was no sign of him, which, she decided, was probably a good thing.

She walked the short distance to the police station. There was a young woman PC at the enquiry desk, who looked up as Rosa approached. She was neat and trim and wearing an engagement ring.

"Can I help you?" she said in a polite but aloof tone.

"I'm Rosa Epton, Mr Scott-Pearce's solicitor. I understand he's been brought here and I'd like to speak to Detective Chief Inspector Harshaw."

The WPC gave Rosa a swift, appraising look before replying.

"I don't think he's available," she said.

"If he's in the station, I wish to

169

see him. Perhaps you'd pass him that message."

"Take a seat and I'll find out if he's in." She turned and disappeared through a door behind her. It was two or three minutes before she came back. Rosa, meanwhile, had remained standing at the counter. "Somebody'll be down from the CID in a moment," the WPC said.

"Does Chief Inspector Harshaw know I'm here?"

"I've just said that somebody'll come and speak to you.

"That isn't an answer to my question."

"I'm not here to answer every question that's put to me," the girl replied tartly and ostentatiously turned her attention to the bundle of forms she had been shuffling when Rosa arrived. "Why don't you go and sit on that bench?" she said, glancing up for a moment.

"Because I prefer to stay where I am."

The WPC shrugged and returned to her forms. About five minutes later, the door behind her opened and a man came through.

"You Ms Epton?" he asked, giving

Rosa a disdainful look.

"Yes, I want to see Chief Inspector Harshaw."

"He's busy. I'm Detective Constable Briggs. What do you want?"

"I think you know very well what I want. I believe you're holding my client, Jeremy Scott-Pearce."

"And if we are?"

"I wish to see him."

"You can't. Not yet, anyway."

"I have a right."

"We also have rights which you lawyers often find it convenient to overlook. You seem to think you can come barging in and make demands at will."

"Am I to understand from that little speech that my client is being interrogated?"

"He was picked up and is being properly interrogated."

"Why wasn't I informed he'd been brought here? Mr Harshaw knows I represent him."

"He came here of his own free will."

"I don't believe you."

Briggs frowned angrily. Each of them was aware that this was shadow boxing in a particularly grey area of the law where judges were often asked to balance the requirements of an investigating officer with those of the person being investigated.

"Is my client under arrest?" Rosa now asked and went on, "Because if he's not, he has every right to leave."

Briggs glared at her. "You'd better hang on," he said, as he turned away.

"Don't worry, I have no intention of leaving."

A further five minutes passed during which time the WPC continued to sort through forms and Rosa remained standing at the counter with an expression of stony determination. Then the door opened once more and Chief Inspector Harshaw appeared.

"Good morning, Miss Epton, except it's afternoon, I think. You've come concerning Mr Scott-Pearce, I understand."

"Is he under arrest?"

"No."

"So he's free to leave immediately?"

"Yes. He's been helping us with our enquiries."

"Spare me the clichés," Rosa said

acerbically. "Have you been interviewing him under caution?"

"Interviewing, yes: under caution, no."

"Did he request my presence?"

"Yes."

"So why didn't you get in touch with me?"

"We certainly should have done so in due course."

"May I see him?" Rosa asked, feeling a trifle deflated by Harshaw's calm, urbane manner.

"Certainly. If you wait here, I'll have him sent down."

"You've finished interviewing him?"

"For the time being. I'm sorry if you've had a wasted journey."

"It need not have been if I'd been able to speak to you this morning. I tried to get through several times."

"I gave instructions that I wasn't to be disturbed. Incidentally, may I enquire how you found out he was here?"

"Somebody saw him being brought into the station and phoned to tell me."

"Somebody being . . . ?"

"Just somebody."

"I see," Harshaw observed thoughtfully.

"What have you been questioning my client about?" Rosa asked.

"Mr Palfrey's death."

"I assumed that. What aspect of his death?"

"A human hair was found on the dead man's jacket that matches the sample of head hair taken from Mr Scott-Pearce. We asked him for an explanation."

"What did he say?" Rosa asked, holding her breath.

"He said it must have got there when he visited the Palfreys about three weeks ago and hung his coat in the closet on top of Mr Palfrey's."

"That sounds very possible."

"Maybe; maybe not."

"Do you have any other evidence that appears to connect my client with the crime?"

"We're still awaiting the results of various forensic tests."

"A single hair isn't much to go on, particularly when there's a plausible explanation."

"People have been convicted on the evidence of a single fingerprint before now," Harshaw said equably.

Rosa was thoughtful for a moment. "Are you absolutely sure Mr Palfrey didn't commit suicide?"

Harshaw sighed. "I can only say that the usual concomitants of suicide are missing. No note of explanation, no prior hint of an intention to take his life, and no apparent reason for doing so."

"Have you found any motive for his murder?"

"Look, Miss Epton, I'm afraid I haven't the time to stand around and be pumped for information," he said with a touch of impatience. "However, I'm glad you're here as it'll save us having to drive Mr Scott-Pearce back to London." He turned to go, but paused at the door. "And, Miss Epton, don't necessarily believe everything he tells you about his interrogation, though I don't expect a solicitor of your experience needs that advice."

Shortly afterwards an ashen-faced Jeremy appeared.

"So the police did eventually let you know I was here," he remarked bitterly, as they left the station and walked to Rosa's car.

"As a matter of fact I heard from another source."

"Do you know I was literally kidnapped outside our flat and forced into a car?" he expostulated.

"I'm afraid the police pulled a fast one. You weren't physically ill-treated, were you?"

"That bloody man Whitehead tried some bully-boy tactics. He'd give the KGB a bad name. I shall get my father to lodge a complaint against him."

"What form did their questioning take?" Rosa asked when they were in the car.

"They tried to get me to confess to Malcolm's death. They took it in turns to shoot questions at me, hoping to trip me up."

"But you didn't admit anything, I hope?"

"Not unless they twist everything I've said. Which I wouldn't put past them."

"Do you recall saying anything that might be turned against you?"

"When you've been bombarded with questions all that time and had words put into your mouth and taken out again, you don't remember what you've said and not said. I kept telling them I wanted my solicitor, but they were just evasive. I feel totally shattered by what I've been through."

His tone was a mixture of petulance and anger, with a clear touch of fear. It was a not unusual cocktail of emotions on the part of someone experiencing a police interrogation. Rosa could only hope that her failure to be present wouldn't prove to be a disaster.

For the time being she didn't see that there was anything to be done save wait for the next move. Even though it would be like sitting in the dark.

* * *

"He was about to crack," Sergeant Whitehead remarked with annoyance. "We'd have had him if his solicitor hadn't come charging in like the cavalry."

Harshaw shrugged. "He's got the wind up and that's good enough for the moment." He glanced at his watch. "It's time Briggs was back. It shouldn't have taken him this long to get to the Palfreys'."

A few minutes later when Harshaw's phone rang, both officers put out a hand to answer it. Harshaw's got there first.

"It's DC Briggs, sir," said a breathless voice. "Mrs Palfrey wasn't in when I arrived and she's only just come back."

"What have you found out?"

"She says that the jacket her husband was wearing when he was shot had been at the cleaners until two days previously. They'd mislaid it and had had it for over a month."

"You didn't tell her why we wanted to know?"

"No, sir."

"Nor that young Scott-Pearce was at the station?"

"No, sir. You told me not to." Brigg's tone was mildly reproachful.

"Where are you phoning from?"

"From Mr Palfrey's study. I thought I'd better call you without delay."

Harshaw pulled a face and turned to Whitehead.

"The good news is that Jeremy Scott-Pearce's hair couldn't have got on the deceased's jacket the way he told us." He paused. "The bad news . . . Well, the bad news depends on whether there are telephone extensions in the Palfrey's house and whether Mrs Palfrey listens in to other people's conversations. I'm not sure how far I trust that lady."

13

COLIN TEARCEY, the Assistant Chief Constable with responsibility for CID operations in the county, had been on sick leave when Malcolm Palfrey met his death, having damaged his back falling off a ladder while painting the upper reaches of his house.

On the day he returned to work a single look at the mass of paper awaiting attention on his desk was sufficient to persuade him that a visit to Nettleford for an on-the-spot briefing from Detective Chief Inspector Harshaw was a priority that shouldn't be neglected.

He had known Palfrey slightly, meeting him from time to time at various functions in the county. They weren't on close terms, but exchanged casual news whenever they met. If the truth be known, neither man particularly liked the other. Nevertheless, the murder of a local solicitor (if murder it was) demanded a measure of special attention. Whatever the public might think of lawyers in general didn't mean that their violent deaths could be passed over in quiet celebration. Moreover, in the absence of the Detective Chief Superintendent who was tied up on a double murder and drugs enquiry at the other end of the county, Tearcey felt it behoved him to be seen out and about taking an interest in Chief Inspector Harshaw's investigation.

"How are you feeling, sir?" Harshaw enquired politely when the Assistant Chief Constable arrived in his office about eleven o'clock on the morning in question, which was two days after the police interview with Jeremy Scott-Pearce.

"Still a bit sore and tender, but I was lucky not to break any bones or even kill myself. I certainly don't recommend falling off ladders." He glanced at Harshaw's desk which was more laden with papers than his own and a good deal less tidy. "So, what's the latest on the Palfrey case, Richard?"

"If it was murder, sir, we're still stuck for a motive. I know we don't have to prove one, but motives are the adhesive that make charges stick."

"Putting aside motives for the moment, what interests me is why Palfrey took a pistol with him when he went out that night. Did he anticipate violence or was he murder bound himself?"

Harshaw nodded. "Another baffling aspect is why did he go to Pan's Place? It's the last place you'd have expected to find him on a December night. If the meeting with whoever it was came about at his instigation, he'd never have suggested such a venue in a hundred years. And if it was the other person's choice, I just can't believe Mr Palfrey would have agreed. He'd have made a counter proposal."

"It's certainly puzzling, which makes me think one must be looking at it from the wrong angle. Also, why did he park his car in a side street some distance away?"

"I suppose he didn't want to run the risk of it being spotted by anyone who knew him."

Tearcey was thoughtful for a while. "It looks as if at some point Palfrey produced his revolver, there was a struggle and

Palfrey was shot. How does that strike you?"

"That would mean accidental death or self-defence, sir."

"It also means that without a motive we're unlikely to bring home a murder charge." Tearcey winced as he shifted in his chair. "Do you still regard young Scott-Pearce as the chief suspect?"

"There's the evidence of the hair, about which he lied."

"That would be enough if we could also prove a motive."

"I've been wondering if he had been having an affair with Mrs Palfrey," Harshaw observed. "I know she's almost twice his age but she's an attractive woman and I've discovered that he often used to call at the house when her husband would have been out. I even began to wonder if he might have been the father of her last child . . . ."

"And?"

"Their respective blood groups are incompatible."

"How did you find that out?"

"The baby had jaundice when he was only a year old and the hospital had a record of his blood group. I was given the information in confidence by one of the consultants who happened to feel beholden to us.

"And of course you already had a sample of Scott-Pearce's blood?"

"Yes."

Tearcey smiled. "Where would we be without the old boy network and the gentle art of bribery? But even if he's not the baby's father, he may still have been having it off with Mrs Palfrey. The thing is, if her husband had discovered, would it have provoked him to murder?"

"I don't think Mr Palfrey was the sort of man who would have shrunk from killing someone, given the right circumstances. He was ruthless and self-centred."

"Most murderers are," Tearcey observed wryly. "However, I'd always gathered he was a devoted family man."

"I think he was probably dutiful rather than devoted. He was a bit of a Victorian in some ways."

"Pity that more parents aren't, then we might have less juvenile crime." After a pause the Assistant Chief Constable went

184

on, "Do you think Mrs Palfrey may know more than she's told us?"

"Still waters run deep," Harshaw remarked cryptically. "She's Italian, sir."

"I knew she was of foreign birth, but thought she came from one of the Slav countries."

"I gather she comes from the part of Italy that adjoins Yugoslavia and has slavonic blood in her veins. She's certainly not your typical Italian."

"How do you describe a typical Italian, Richard?" Tearcey enquired with an amused expression.

"Non-stop talking and gesticulating, that sort of thing."

"Ah!" The Assistant Chief Constable gazed about him and winced again as he shifted his position. "Apart from young Scott-Pearce, anyone else in the frame? I've heard that Palfrey and his partner weren't on good terms. Anything to that?"

"It was common knowledge in Nettleford, sir. Certainly there's no sign of Mr Chance going into mourning over his partner's death."

"Is it possible he'd been sticking his

finger in the till and that Palfrey had found out?"

"Possible, sir, but no evidence to prove it."

"That could be because we haven't probed deep enough."

"It would mean calling in accountants, sir, and we've no cause to do that. We can't go burrowing into the firm's accounts without justification, particularly as we'd be searching for a motive rather than evidence of murder."

"I suppose not," Tearcey said and winced again as he put his hand up to his face.

"If only we could find a motive," Harshaw went on. "A motive would almost certainly lead us to the murderer."

"Have you talked to Mr Palfrey's secretary, Miss Whatshername? She'd know who might have had a motive."

"Miss Seeberg. She's quite sure that Mr Chance killed her employer. She's not said so in precise words, but she's made her feelings pretty clear. She was a devoted secretary to Mr Palfrey, but took no trouble to get on with anyone else in the office."

186

"What about this man, Thorn? I'm not sure why you've given him such long odds in the suspect stakes. After all, he alone can be said to have had a motive."

"I know that, sir, but I still don't believe he did it. Anyway, he has an alibi of sorts."

"One provided by his wife who says they went to bed early that night. In any event he didn't have to be out very late to have been able to commit this crime."

"His wife also says, sir, that he didn't leave the house after coming in around six o'clock."

"Wives often loyally support their husbands' alibis. It's part of the marriage contract in some sections of society. Anyway, I gather he spent most of his evenings in the pub, so why wasn't he there that particular evening?"

"He had an upset stomach."

Tearcey made a scornful sound. "It would take more than an upset stomach to keep the likes of Thorn out of the boozer. I'd have thought it was worth pulling him in again and testing his story further."

Harshaw looked unconvinced. "But why on earth should Thorn and Mr Palfrey meet at Pan's Place?"

"Thorn could have lured him there by some pretence or other and Palfrey took the precaution of going armed."

"Why'd he go at all?"

"All right, you put up some ideas and I'll shoot them down," Tearcey said in a tone of mild irritation.

"I'm sorry, sir, I didn't mean — "

"No apology required. I was only peering up every possible avenue."

"Believe me, sir, I've peered up them all until my eyes are ready to drop out."

"So what do you propose next?"

"It seems to me that all I can do is to continue turning over stones until we get a lead. I still hope the lab will come up with something further."

"I'll see if I can get them to hurry things along."

"The trouble is that the lab people like to be given an idea what they should be looking for and I've not been able to offer them any help."

The Assistant Chief Constable was

silent for a while. Then he said in a thoughtful voice, "It's significant that Scott-Pearce lied to you about how his hair got on to Palfrey's jacket."

Harshaw nodded. "Significant, but not one hundred per cent damning. Moreover, the next time I see him, it'll have to be in the presence of his solicitor and that's not going to make things any easier."

"I expect you know that his father and Palfrey were in cahoots at one time. Business deals and the like. I don't know what their relationship has been latterly." He let out a sigh. "Well, provided I can get out of this chair, I'd better be on my way, Richard. Meanwhile keep me in touch with developments.

After escorting the Assistant Chief Constable to his car, Harshaw returned to his office in a morose mood.

★ ★ ★

Rosa washed up her supper dishes and sat down to enjoy a wildlife programme on television about meerkats. She had seen it once before and been entranced

189

by these captivating animals who had created a disciplined and caring society for themselves. The manner in which they would sit bolt upright and scan their surroundings with alert expressions was infinitely memorable. When the programme was over she decided that she had enjoyed it even more the second time.

It had not long been finished when her door phone buzzed. She wasn't expecting any visitors and wondered who could be calling at that hour. Though not late, she didn't normally receive unannounced visits in the evening. As she went into the hall to find out who it was at the front door below, she thought it more than likely that it was somebody wanting one of the other flats in the house.

"Hello, who is it?" she said, lifting the receiver from its bracket on the wall.

"Tom Berry," a voice crackled back at her. "May I come up?"

Rosa hesitated a second as her heart gave a wild thump, then said, "Yes."

She pressed the button that released the catch on the entrance door and stood waiting beside her own front door listening to the approaching footsteps. Her flat was on the third floor and there was no lift. Unlike most of her visitors, Tom Berry seemed to be taking the stairs two at a time. Then her own doorbell rang, which made her jump. She counted up to five to give the impression she had come from the furthest reaches to open the door.

Tom Berry stood there with the faintly enigmatic expression she had come to associate with him. He was wearing a black leather jacket over an open-neck green and white striped shirt and a pair of bottle green cords.

"Hello," he said, "I hope it's all right to call, but I happened to be passing." He gave her a solemn wink in case she was inclined to accept the improbability of this explanation.

"Yes, come on in," Rosa said in as natural a voice as she could muster.

"Very cosy," he remarked as he gazed round her small living room.

"Would you like something to drink?" she enquired.

"I'd love a cup of tea," he said, turning

191

his gaze on her. "I make it a rule not to drink and drive. I saw too many mangled bodies pulled from wrecked cars when I was at the hospital."

"I'll go and put the kettle on," she said as she pushed past him to go to the kitchen.

He followed her and stood in the doorway watching her as she went about filling the kettle and fetching cups and saucers from the cupboard and milk from the fridge.

"Did you ever see that TV programme about meerkats?" she enquired, feeling a need to keep the conversation at an innocuous level. "It was on again this evening."

"We could do with a few meerkats as look-outs in Shilman Green park. What people get up to there is nobody's business. Apart from murder, that is."

The tea made, Rosa carried the tray into the living room.

"Where would you like to sit?" she asked.

"Why don't we both sit on the sofa?"

As she poured the tea she could feel the warmth of his body next to her.

He had taken off his leather jacket and his short-sleeved shirt revealed nicely browned arms.

"I know something I wanted to ask you," she said quickly. "How did you recognise Jeremy Scott-Pearce when you saw him being taken into the police station?"

"I'd seen his photo in the local paper."

Rosa frowned. "I wasn't aware it had appeared in the press."

"If you really want to know, I recognised him as someone I'd seen in the park."

"When?"

"Oh, back in the summer."

"Have you disclosed that to the police?"

"No. Would you sooner I didn't?"

For heaven's sake be careful how you answer that, a lawyer's inner voice warned Rosa.

"It's not for me to advise you what and what not to tell the police," she said. "It would be improper."

"Why?"

"Because you're clearly a witness for the prosecution if the matter ever comes to court, and I could be on the other side."

"Only if your client's involved."

"Wait a minute!" she exclaimed. "If you recognised the person being led into the police station as someone you'd once seen in the park, that wouldn't have told you his name. How did you know that?"

He stared at her impassively for several seconds.

"That's a good point," he said at length.

"But it doesn't answer my question."

He put down his cup and saucer and pulled Rosa gently into his side.

"You know, just as I know, that we clicked the very first time we set eyes on one another, so why don't we use my visit to become better acquainted?"

Before Rosa could think of a reply, he was kissing her and she was kissing him back.

"We mustn't," she said hoarsely, easing herself away.

"Why not? Didn't you like me kissing you?"

"It's not that. It's . . . "

"It was a lovely kiss. And don't forget it takes two to kiss just as it does to tango."

With that he leaned over and kissed her again, as Rosa's head swam with a confusion of thoughts.

"Just relax," he whispered when the kiss was over. "What's it matter that you're a solicitor and I'm a park-keeper or that I'm a few years younger than you? It's immaterial. Anyway, I get the impression you're not averse to what we're doing, so relax. You're not married, are you?" Rosa shook her head. "And you don't have a live-in boyfriend by the look of things, so why not let me make love to you? I'm pretty good at it with the right girl . . . "

Ninety minutes later they returned to the living room with a fresh pot of tea. To Rosa in her bemused state the tea managed somehow to give the incident a domestic touch. Meanwhile, pleasure, guilt and alarm fought for supremacy in her whirling thoughts.

"You still haven't told me how you knew my client's name," she said in a shaky voice, making a grab at normality.

He gave a cheerful laugh. "If you insist on knowing, we met in a pub. We were both on our own and got talking and exchanged names. Now are you satisfied?" He glanced at his watch. "I'll have to be going soon. I've enjoyed our evening and I like to think that you have, too, if you can bring yourself to admit it." He gave her a wry smile. "I probably know more about hang-ups than you do. I was half-way to becoming a doctor before I had my breakdown, so I've seen both sides of the coin." He got up and stood for a moment looking down at Rosa. "I'll keep in touch and let you know if I hear anything of interest. I can see myself out. Thanks for everything." He bent down and gave her a quick kiss. The next moment he had gone and she heard the front door slam.

For several minutes she sat trying to analyse her thoughts. She had never before met anybody quite like Tom Berry. For someone who had a mental breakdown, he was alarmingly self-assured. His calm effrontery had combined with his good looks to mesmerise her. She could envisage him as a pretty child and there were still vestiges of prettiness in his face, in particular the shape of his mouth and his steady hazel-coloured eyes. She had always been vulnerable to a certain type of young man, but he had swept all before him. And to think she had only met him by the merest chance.

A sudden shattering thought burst in her head. Supposing he was involved in some way with Malcolm Palfrey's death? Then his visit could be seen as a calculated act with an ulterior motive, even though his love-making lacked nothing in joyous spontaneity.

She realised there was no point in her going to bed and hoping to fall asleep. Her mind was in far too great a turmoil.

While one half of her hoped there would be no occasion to see him again, the other half felt weak with excitement at the prospect.

14

THOUGH Rosa was in court both morning and afternoon the next day, she was thankful that neither of her cases would require any special effort of concentration.

Memory of what had happened the previous evening haunted her like an hypnotic dream, and yet there had been a certain inevitability about the course of events.

She had not long returned to her office when the door opened and Robin appeared.

"We've been a bit like ships that pass in the night the last few days," he remarked amiably. "I thought I'd find out how things are going in your Nettleford case?"

"There've been no further developments since the police interrogated Jeremy Scott-Pearce," she said with a frail smile.

"Are they likely to charge him?"

"I'm sure they'd like to."

"If they do it simply on the evidence of the hair they found, you should have a good run for your money. Indeed, the case might even be thrown out on a submission of no case to answer. That is, if defending counsel can cast doubt on the lab's finding."

"I imagine they're already seeking advice from the CPS."

Robin peered at Rosa with a faintly worried expression. "Are you feeling all right? You don't sound your usual zestful self."

"I think I may have picked up a bug."

"There's a lot of flu around. If you don't feel better tomorrow, I'd take a couple of days off. Better to nip these viral infections in the bud rather than struggle on feeling awful and spreading your germs."

"I'll see how I am in the morning."

"Have you heard anything from the court about the outstanding charge being reinstated in the list?"

"Nothing."

"The logical thing would be for Chance

to take over Amanda Ritchie's defence."

"I've no idea whether Chance was on better terms with Ritchie than he was with Malcolm Palfrey. Anyway, Amanda was Palfrey's godchild."

"What's that got to do with anything?"

"Probably nothing," Rosa said, wishing Robin would depart and leave her to cope with the cross-currents of her thoughts.

"I suggest you go home now," Robin said firmly. "And don't come in tomorrow unless you're feeling better. You're not in court tomorrow, are you?"

"No."

"All the more reason to stay in bed with a couple of hot water-bottles. I'm sure Susan would come up and minister to your needs. In fact, I know she would."

"No, I'll be all right," Rosa said. Fond as she was of Robin's wife, she certainly didn't want her driving up from their home near Windsor with flasks of nourishing broth.

"I don't think Rosa's feeling very well," Robin remarked to Stephanie as he passed her command post on the way back to his own room. "Probably picked up a virus."

Stephanie who had her own view of Rosa's malaise offered no comment though her eyes reflected wry amusement. She had known Rosa long enough to be able to recognise the difference between a flu germ and one of Cupid's untimely arrows. Not that she would have expected the senior partner of Snaith and Epton to share her talent for diagnosis. She also had the added advantage of remembering the telephone call Rosa had received from the park-keeper at Shilman Green. Trained telephonists were able to interpret vocal nuances that others wouldn't notice. She was fond of Rosa and it wasn't the first time she had witnessed her emotions looping the loop.

Rosa decided to take Robin's advice and go home early. She filled her briefcase with papers to read in the quiet of her own living room and departed from the office under Stephanie's sardonic gaze.

Around five-thirty her phone rang and for several seconds she stared at it in uncertainty. What if it were Tom Berry? She wasn't in the right mood to hear from him. On the other hand she knew that the sound of his voice would paralyse her will.

In the event it was not Tom but Jeremy Scott-Pearce on the other end of the line. He sounded tense and from the background noises he was in a public call box.

"I phoned your office, but they said you'd gone home," he said. "I have to see you urgently. Is tomorrow morning all right?"

"Yes, but what's happened?"

"I can't explain on the phone. What time shall I come?"

"Ten o'clock suit you?"

"I'll be there."

"The police haven't been in touch again, have they?"

"No. See you in the morning." He rang off before Rosa could say anything further.

She was left to wonder where he had been calling from and what was the sudden urgency. He had sounded fraught and not far from breaking-point.

★ ★ ★

Stephanie gave Rosa a quick appraising look when she arrived in the office shortly after nine o'clock the next morning.

"Mr Jeremy Scott-Pearce phoned after you'd left yesterday afternoon," she said.

"I know. He called me at home."

"I didn't give him your number," Stephanie said defensively.

"He probably looked it up in the book. Did he say where he was ringing from?"

"No, but it was definitely a call box."

"That was my impression, too. He's coming to the office this morning." She glanced at her watch. "Around ten."

"How are you feeling today?" Stephanie said as Rosa turned to go to her room.

"Better, thank you, Steph."

Stephanie's small secret smile told Rosa that whoever else she might fool, it would never be their indispensable office receptionist.

It was some forty minutes later that she announced Jeremy's arrival and Rosa went to her door to greet him.

He had a fraught air as he came in and sat down in Rosa's visitor's chair. Or to be more exact, perched himself on its forward edge.

"Would you like a cup of coffee?" Rosa asked.

He shook his head, then began fiddling with his lower lip as if trying to remould it. Suddenly he looked up and met Rosa's gaze.

"I've come to make a confession."

"A confession to what?"

"To having been involved in Malcolm Palfrey's death."

Rosa could not but note his careful choice of words.

"Before you go any further," she broke in quickly, "I ought to warn you that if you're about to tell me you were responsible for his death and the case comes for trial, I couldn't argue that you had nothing to do with it, which is what you've told me hitherto. You do understand that?"

"Yes," he said with a touch of impatience.

"And is it your intention to go to the police?"

"Yes."

Rosa drew a deep breath. "OK, go ahead."

"I killed him in self-defence," he said bleakly. "He drew his pistol and was going to shoot me. We had a struggle and the pistol went off and killed him. That in a nutshell is what happened."

★ ★ ★

"Whose finger was on the trigger at the time?"

"I suppose it must have been mine."

Rosa pursed her lips. So far it was a confession couched in circumlocution. After a pause, she said, "I suggest you start at the beginning and tell me how you and Mr Palfrey came to meet in Pan's Place that evening. That is, if you still want to tell me."

"He phoned me in the morning and said it was vitally important that we met before the case the next day. He wouldn't tell me why, but said secrecy was necessary as he was no longer representing me and it mustn't become known. He stressed that on no account should I tell you. I asked him where he proposed we should meet and he said Pan's Place in the park at Shilman Green — "

"What was your reaction to that?"

"I asked him why such a godforsaken place, but he said he had his reasons. I asked him again why he wanted to see me, and why all the secrecy, but he said he didn't wish to go into details on the phone — "

"Do you know where he was calling from?"

"No idea. Could have been his office: could have been home."

"What time did he phone you?"

"Around nine o'clock."

"On Wednesday morning?"

"Yes."

"Go on."

"If it had been anyone other than Malcolm, I'd never have agreed to go." He gave a helpless shrug. "But I've known him all my life and he's always been a sort of uncle figure to me, so I felt I should go along with his wishes, however bizarre."

"What did you think he wanted?"

"I wracked my brains, but couldn't think of anything that made sense. Anyway, I drove down to Shilman Green on Wednesday evening — he'd asked me to be there at nine-thirty — left the car and entered the park. It was completely dark apart from a single lamp half-way along the path that bisects it. There was no light in the area of Pan's Place and the closer I got, the more nervous I became. I was also suspicious and wildly curious. I remember whistling to give myself a bit of Dutch courage. When I arrived at the gap in the bushes that leads into Pan's Place, I called out, 'Are you there, Malcolm?' and he called back, 'It's OK, I'm here.' I pushed my way through and I could make out Malcolm sitting on one of the benches. By that time, my eyes had become more accustomed to the dark. He stood up almost immediately and I could see he had something in his right hand. 'I'm glad you've come, I've got something for you,' he said and raised his right arm."

Jeremy's voice had become taut and his face glistened with sweat as he re-lived events. "I then realised he was pointing a gun straight at me. If I'd turned and made a dash he'd have shot me in the back before I'd gone a yard. So I put my head down and butted him in the stomach. It was presumably the last thing he was expecting because he let out a grunt and dropped the gun. We then had a sort of crazy wrestling match, each of us groping for the pistol. I managed to pick it up and while we continued to struggle, it suddenly went off and he collapsed on the bench behind him. I could see he had a wound in the head and appeared to be dead. I just turned and ran. I got back to my car and drove home faster than I've ever driven."

His voice had become quite hoarse and he looked utterly exhausted. No wonder, Rosa reflected, that he had appeared a wreck when they met at the court the next morning. What he had just described would have been infinitely more traumatic than the effects of a bad prawn in a Chinese takeaway.

"Did you ever discover why he'd lured you to Pan's Place?" Rosa asked.

"No."

"But you must have some idea?"

"I haven't."

"He got you there in order to murder you; you must have some thoughts as to his motive?"

Jeremy gave a distracted shake of the

head. "Perhaps he thought I had found out something about him and presented a threat."

"And had you?"

"No."

"What might you have found out that could have made him feel menaced?"

"I haven't a clue." After a pause he went on, "A lot of people have skeletons in their cupboards and I'm sure Malcolm was no exception, but I wasn't aware of any. I wasn't someone to whom he'd have told his secrets."

"It would have to be a particularly threatening skeleton to push somebody into committing murder in order to keep it dark. Can't you think of anything? For example, might you unwittingly have given him the impression that you knew something to his disadvantage? Think back to when he was still representing you. I presume you saw him a number of times during that period?"

"Only twice, I think."

"Could it be anything to do with his sudden refusal to go on defending you?"

"How do you mean?"

"I don't really know, I was just thinking aloud, but he did throw you overboard rather abruptly."

"He said it was because Amanda was determined to put all the blame on me."

"I know, and that created a conflict of interest. Incidentally, did Amanda give you any explanation when you saw her in court?"

"No. I didn't ask her and, anyway, I was feeling terrible. Everyone was dashing about wondering what had happened to Malcolm and where he was, and all the time I knew." He shivered. "It was like a bad nightmare."

Rosa was thoughtful and almost a minute passed before she spoke again.

"What's made you decide to speak out?"

"Things have been preying on my mind ever since his death and the strain became too much."

"Have you discussed matters with your father?"

He shook his head. "You're the first person I've told."

"I think you should talk to your father before any further steps are taken."

"No."

"He's bound to hear if the police charge you."

Jeremy bit his lip. "It'll be too late then for him to try and argue me out of my decision."

"And your mother, have you spoken to her?"

"No." He glanced at Rosa and it was as if he read her mind. "You won't be able to get in touch with Dad because he's travelling around in Italy at the moment."

"When'll he be back?"

"Not for several days. Are the police likely to charge me immediately?"

"I can't answer that. They might, they might not."

"And if they do, what with?"

"Probably murder."

He gave a small shiver. "How can you say it was murder?"

"I didn't say you'd be convicted of murder. Indeed, if the court accepts your story, you stand a good chance of getting off altogether."

"There'll be no problem about bail, will there?"

"It's still the exception in murder cases, but your prospects are better than most." She gave him a thoughtful stare before going on. "Where were you speaking from when you called me at home last night?"

"Why?" he asked with a sudden frown.

"Because there was a lot of background noise of movement and people talking."

The question seemed to throw him momentarily off balance.

"Oh . . . er . . . yes, I remember now. I was in a call box in the King's Road. Our telephone at home was temporarily on the blink."

Liar, Rosa thought. But why? And how many less obvious lies have you told me while you've been sitting in that chair?

15

BEFORE he left her office, Rosa insisted that what he was proposing to tell the police should be put in the form of a written statement.

"It's better," she said, "that we go armed with your statement and hand it to Chief Inspector Harshaw, rather than let the police put it into writing. They have ways of slanting things and if Sergeant Whitehead takes it down, we could have a running battle."

She wondered if at this point he might say that he had changed his mind; didn't want to go near the police; and, moreover, that what he had told her was all lies. He didn't do so, however, and readily agreed to her proposal. Rosa roughed out a statement and told him to make any corrections he wanted before doing a fair copy in his own hand.

The statement began: "I, Jeremy Scott-Pearce, am making this statement of my own free will, in the knowledge that it may be used in evidence in any proceedings against me . . . " He signed it at the end and Rosa added her own signature.

"Right," she said, "the next step is to make an appointment to see Chief Inspector Harshaw. We ought to do that as soon as possible. We don't want anyone asking why there was an interval between the making of the statement and it being handed to the police."

Jeremy licked his lips nervously and gave a brief nod and Rosa reached for her telephone.

"Get me Detective Chief Inspector Harshaw at Nettleford police station, will you, Steph?"

A few seconds later her phone gave a peremptory buzz and she lift the receiver.

"Mr Harshaw? It's Rosa Epton . . . I have Mr Jeremy Scott-Pearce in my office and we'd like to come and see you as soon as possible. Would two o'clock this afternoon be convenient? Mr Scott-Pearce has something important to say to the police . . . yes, it concerns Mr Palfrey's death . . . Right, we'll see you then." She replaced the receiver. "That's fixed then," she said.

It wasn't surprising that Jeremy wore an anxious expression for now the die was cast. Any reneging would be more than difficult to explain. She herself still felt uneasy that his father remained in ignorance of what was happening. If, in due course, it was she who had to phone Geneva and tell him that his son had been charged with homicide and was in custody, she could anticipate an outraged response. Nevertheless, Jeremy was nearly twenty-two and was a fully-fledged adult in the eyes of the law, not that Rosa thought Charles Scott-Pearce would be mollified by such a reminder.

Leaving him in her office, she hurried along to Robin's room to tell him what had happened.

"How are you feeling today?" he enquired as she appeared.

For a second Rosa was puzzled, then remembered the circumstances of her departure the previous afternoon. "Oh . . . er. . . yes, I seem to have shaken off whatever bug it was. But I wanted to tell you the latest in the Scott-Pearce saga."

Robin listened in attentive silence while she told him what had happened.

"What a very curious business," he remarked when she finished. "From what you'd told me about him, it seems out of character. Confessions and getting things off his chest, I mean. On the other hand I can't see why he should say what he has if it's not true. Staying mum would have been an easier option."

"Of course his statement will hardly help the police to prove murder," Rosa observed.

"I agree." He gave Rosa a wry smile. "They may well end up wishing you'd stayed away from their doorstep."

Ten minutes later Rosa and Jeremy were on their way to Nettleford in Rosa's car, his signed statement lodged in her briefcase like an explosive device of unknown power.

★ ★ ★

The statement lay on the desk between them. Chief Inspector Harshaw had read it with the air of someone who

216

had been handed a report he found mildly interesting. He pushed it over to Sergeant Whitehead who read it to an accompaniment of derisive noises.

"This document was prepared in your office, I gather, Miss Epton?" Harshaw remarked.

"Yes. After my client had told me what you've just read in his statement, I said it would be best to commit it to writing there and then."

At this, Sergeant Whitehead made the sort of sound with which members of parliament are inclined to greet their opponents' views.

Pretending not to notice, Harshaw said, "I should like to ask your client a few questions, Miss Epton. You've no objection, I hope?"

"Under caution?"

Harshaw bit his lip. "Yes," he said reluctantly.

"Ask away and I'll advise my client whether or not to answer each question as it comes."

Harshaw recited the caution with as much expression as a weary priest giving absolution and went on, "My

217

first question, Mr Scott-Pearce, is why has it taken you so long to come forward with this account of events?"

It was an awkward but unavoidable question and Rosa gave Jeremy a nod, indicating that he should answer it.

"I was in a state of shock afterwards and became scared when the full realisation of what had happened sank in."

"Not too shocked or scared to tell us a string of lies when we interviewed you," Whitehead broke in.

"That's not a question," Rosa said firmly. "And even if you turned it into one, I would still advise my client not to answer it."

"And may I ask why not?" Whitehead said in a hectoring tone.

"Because it invites argument and not a plain answer."

Harshaw, who had listened to the exchange without reaction, now leaned forward and said, "When did you have a change of mind and decide to make a statement?"

"I finally decided yesterday, though I had been working up to it ever since you interviewed me."

"And so you got in touch with Miss Epton?"

"Yes and went to her office this morning and told her what now appears in the statement. As soon as it was written we drove here."

"Has anyone exerted pressure on you to make the statement?"

"No. I made it of my own free will."

"I note it says that. And it's the truth?"

"Yes."

Harshaw looked thoughtful for a moment, while Sergeant Whitehead sat with a glowering expression.

"I note that you say your finger was on the trigger when the pistol went off. If that was so, how did you avoid leaving a fingerprint?"

"I was wearing gloves. I always wear them for driving. Those thin backless ones."

Harshaw raised a sceptical eyebrow. "A bit unusual for a young man like yourself to wear gloves for driving?"

"I do so on medical advice. I have a skin allergy which oil and grease produces. You only have to look at my car to realise the risks."

It was a good answer and clearly not one that Harshaw had been expecting. His question about the absence of a fingerprint had revealed an openness of mind on his part that was plainly not shared by Sergeant Whitehead. Rosa could see that the statement had put the police in something of a dilemma. In one sense it solved their crime, though hardly in the manner they expected or, in the case of Sergeant Whitehead, wanted. On the other hand they were not in a position to reject it as a pack of lies, for they had no evidence that it was. Voluntary statements by defendants invariably form part of the prosecution case, even if they don't support it one hundred per cent. As far as the police were concerned, the value of Jeremy's statement was that it amounted to an admission of responsibility for Malcolm Palfrey's death, albeit in circumstances of self-defence.

Harshaw, who had ostensibly been re-reading the statement, now looked up and said, "I'll be glad, Miss Epton, if you and your client will go and wait in another room while I get in touch with my superiors."

It was apparent from his expression that Sergeant Whitehead would have preferred to escort them to the cells rather than to the cheerless room along the corridor, the door of which he flung open to admit them and then closed with an unnecessary bang.

"What's going to happen now?" Jeremy asked nervously when he and Rosa were alone.

"They're deciding whether to charge you."

"Do you think they will?"

"If they do, I doubt whether it'll be Chief Inspector Harshaw's decision. I don't think he's too happy with the way things have turned out."

"Too bad! The police never did like the truth if it thwarts their hopes. No second guess needed to know what that bastard Whitehead would like to do." Rosa was silent and, after a pause, Jeremy went on, "If they don't charge me, will that mean we're free to go?"

"Yes, though it's possible they'll bail you to return here in a couple of weeks when they'll either have to charge you or let you go."

"Can they do that?"

"Yes. It's a provision that's used when their enquiries don't justify a charge being immediately preferred."

Jeremy pulled a face. "Sounds a typical police ploy. Everything's loaded in their favour."

"Not really, and *they* certainly don't think so. Anyway, better that than to find yourself in immediate custody."

"But you said I had a good chance of getting bail," he exclaimed.

"If they charge you today, you'll be kept in custody until you appear in court tomorrow. That's when I'll apply for bail and, with luck, it'll be granted."

"But even if I am charged, can't I have bail immediately?"

"In theory you could. In practice the police'll refuse to consider it. They'll almost certainly oppose it in court as well. They'll stress the seriousness of the charge, the fact you might abscond and the temptation you'll be under to interfere with witnesses — "

"What witnesses?" he broke in angrily.

"I don't even know any of the so-called witnesses. Anyway, I was the only witness."

"Just keep calm," Rosa said. "It merely happens to be one of the standard objections to bail."

In the silence that followed, Rosa reflected on the dilemma in which she had been placed or, to be more honest, in which she had allowed herself to be placed.

Fortunately, before she could become too introspective, the door opened and Sergeant Whitehead appeared. He jerked his head indicating that they should follow him.

Chief Inspector Harshaw was sitting at his desk just as they had left him. Clearing his throat, he said in an almost brusque tone, "Pending further enquiries, Mr Scott-Pearce, you will be bailed to return here two weeks from today." He glanced at Rosa. "Does your client understand the position, Miss Epton?"

"Yes, I'd already explained it to him."

"Good. Then once the formalities have been completed, you're free to go." As Sergeant Whitehead took Jeremy off to sign the necessary forms, Harshaw turned to Rosa and remarked, "A clever statement, if I may say so, Miss Epton. It purports to say a lot, but it's what it doesn't say that really interests me."

"I'm afraid my client doesn't have all the answers."

"But somebody has, Miss Epton. Somebody has."

16

AS soon as Rosa and Jeremy had departed, Chief Inspector Harshaw phoned Nadine Palfrey and said that he wished to see her as soon as possible. What he didn't say was that he wanted to talk to her before Jeremy Scott-Pearce got in touch with her. Maybe he wouldn't try to do so, but Harshaw was taking no chances. He informed Sergeant Whitehead where he was going and added firmly that he proposed taking WPC Perkins with him as he had on the previous occasion. Since then he had found out that her first name was Elaine and that she had a social science degree from Southampton University. Having himself entered the police with the minimum educational qualification required at the time, he was intrigued and, at times, daunted by the intellectual talent the force was now able to attract. As for WPC Perkins he found her a pleasant, composed dumpling of a girl who didn't seek to give him an inferiority complex.

She was waiting for him by the car when he got downstairs.

"I gather we're off to see Mrs Palfrey again, sir," she remarked as they drove out of the station yard.

Harshaw nodded and told her the reason for the visit.

"Let's hope she's more forthcoming this time. I'm still certain she was holding things back when we saw her previously. Did she say anything when you told her you wished to see her?"

"Only that she'd be at home. She's not a woman to give much away unless she wants to."

It took them fifteen minutes to reach Kingsmere Farm. Lights shone from every window and WPC Perkins parked the car just beyond the front porch.

The door was opened by Cressida who stared at them in surprise.

"Oh! I thought it was the car that takes me to my ballet classes," she said.

"I'm afraid not. We've come to see your mother. She's expecting us."

226

At that moment Nadine appeared in the hall.

"Please come in," she said. Turning to her daughter, she went on, "I'm sure it'll be here in a moment. Why not wait by the door and you'll hear it arrive."

Cressida pulled a face. "It was late last time and Miss Anders was furious." Turning to the officers she said, "We're rehearsing a scene from Swan Lake." She pulled another face. "I find all those swans a bit silly ... There's the car now! Bye, Mummy!"

Nadine led the way into the living room where they seemed to seat themselves automatically as they had done on the officers' previous visit.

"There's been a fresh development, Mrs Palfrey," Harshaw said, watching her closely. "Jeremy Scott-Pearce has confessed to killing your husband."

Her head lifted as that of an animal sensing danger and her right hand gripped the arm of her chair.

"He couldn't have killed Malcolm. What possible motive could he have had?"

"He says it was in self-defence."

227

"Self-defence? What are you saying?"

"That your husband tried to kill him."

"That's equally absurd."

"It's what Jeremy says. Do you think he's lying?"

She gave a helpless shrug. "I just don't know what to say."

"I want you to think back to the evening your husband met his death. What exactly did he tell you before he left the house?"

"That he had to meet somebody, but wouldn't be out long."

"Are you sure he gave you no clue as to whom he was going to meet?"

"Quite sure."

"And you never asked?"

"No. Malcolm didn't like being questioned about his movements. If he wanted me to know things, he told me."

"How did he seem when he went out that evening?"

"You have asked me all this before and I have told you," she said with an impatient shrug.

"Tell me again."

"He was just his ordinary self."

"Not tense or excited?"

"No."

"Perfectly calm?"

"Yes."

"Of course we now know that he was armed when he left the house, did he look like someone setting out to commit murder?"

For several seconds, Nadine stared at Harshaw without replying. Then she said coldly, "I've never seen anyone setting out to commit a murder, so I wouldn't know. Perhaps, Chief Inspector, you can tell me what I should look for." A moment later she added, "I'm sorry, I shouldn't have said that, but the very idea that my husband might have wanted to murder someone just isn't credible."

"What I would like to know is what motive he had," Harshaw went on in a musing tone, then added, "Did he ever object to your friendship with Jeremy Scott-Pearce?"

"Why should he have? Jeremy regarded me as a big sister. As you probably know he's never been very close to his mother and I filled that gap." She looked up and met Harshaw's gaze. "Let me make it quite clear, my friendship with Jeremy never extended to the bedroom. You must accept my word that I was never unfaithful to Malcolm all the time I was married to him."

"Or he to you?"

"I would not have tolerated it."

"What would you have done if you'd discovered he was having an affair with another woman?"

"I suppose you want me to say I'd have killed him?"

"Well, would you?"

"You obviously believe that all women from latin countries kill their husbands at the first hint of unfaithfulness. It's true they may be more volatile than English women, but they can also be deeply forgiving."

"Does that mean you ever had occasion to forgive your husband for straying from the straight and narrow path?"

"Perhaps."

"Will you tell me about it?"

"It was when I was expecting Cressida. He had a brief affair with Mrs Chance. So brief, in fact, that you could scarcely call it an affair. More a quick romp which

Malcolm immediately regretted. Clare Chance has always been apt to make passes at other women's husbands."

"How did you find out?"

"There's always someone waiting to pass on that sort of news."

"Did Mr Chance know?"

She shrugged. "I've no idea. Maybe he prefers not to know what his wife gets up to."

"Anyway, that was all of twelve years ago?" She nodded. "Did your husband know that you found out?"

"I made sure that he did. I didn't wish him to do it again."

"And as far as you know, he never did?"

"No."

Harshaw was thoughtful. "Was your husband with you when your son was born last year?"

She unclasped, then re-clasped her hands as if the question embarrassed her.

"No. I was visiting relatives at the time and Crispin was born prematurely. I didn't have time to get back to England, it all happened so suddenly. And now he'll never know his father," she added in a small, sad voice, as a tear rolled down her cheek.

It seemed to Harshaw that the interview had not taken them much further forward. Apart from learning that Malcolm Palfrey had been unfaithful to his wife some twelve years before, nothing fresh had emerged. Certainly nothing that answered the questions that still surrounded his death.

"What do you make of her now?" he asked WPC Perkins as they started on the drive back.

"You need to get up early in the morning, sir, to catch her out. She's as tough as boot leather. I know she shed a little tear when she spoke of her son growing up without a father, but even the Empress Messalina could produce a tear at required moments."

"You don't think her emotions are more than skin-deep?"

"What does occur to me, sir, is that we have only her word about her husband going out to meet someone on the evening of his death?"

"Do you believe she's lying about that?"

"If she played some part in his death, she'd have a reason to lie."

"You certainly have a low opinion of the lady," Harshaw remarked thoughtfully.

"I'm still quite sure she hasn't told us as much as she could," WPC Perkins said. "Absolutely sure, in fact," she added, in case her message hadn't been understood.

★ ★ ★

News of Jeremy's visit to the police station was bound to get around in any event, but with Detective Sergeant Whitehead determined to leak it, the ripples soon reached out.

Austin Fulwood, who was Palfrey and Co.'s outdoor clerk, got it straight from the horse's mouth on his way back to the office from court. He had been with the firm almost as long as Madge Seeberg, not that time had made them bosom friends.

Miss Seeberg was now working as a supernumerary in the small typing pool, Adrian Chance having made it clear it was either that or being given a month's

233

notice. She had been obliged to swallow her pride, though it had brought a further chill to her relationship with the new head of the firm.

"Here, listen to this," Austin Fulwood said as he swept into the room, where she happened to be alone at that moment. "Young Scott-Pearce has been at the police station most of the afternoon and has confessed to killing Mr Palfrey."

"Where did you hear that?" Miss Seeberg asked suspiciously.

"Happened to meet Sergeant Whitehead just now and he told me."

"Has he been charged?"

"He's been given police bail."

"If he's confessed, why hasn't he been charged?"

"It seems he tried to make out that it was self-defence."

Miss Seeberg was thoughtful for a moment. "Does he know yet?" she asked, indicating Adrian Chance's room with a sinuous movement of her head.

"He's out." After a pause, he went on, "Well, what do you think?"

"I think the police are fools. They're taking the easy option."

"But he's confessed," Fulwood said, nettled by her negative reaction to his item of hot news.

"So I heard you say."

"What do you mean then, easy option?"

"People don't always make true confessions," Miss Seeberg said. "As often as not they have ulterior motives for giving statements to the police."

"So what was young Scott-Pearce's ulterior motive?" Fulwood asked with a faint sneer.

"I prefer to keep my opinions to myself," Miss Seeberg said loftily and turned back to her typewriter.

"Well, if you ask me, his conscience got the better of him. He couldn't go on living with himself knowing what he'd done. Anyway, the sooner it's all cleared up, the better for all of us."

But Miss Seeberg was not to be drawn.

★ ★ ★

Amanda Ritchie had once thought she could fall in love with Jeremy, but that had been two or three years ago. She had tried to seduce him, but without success. This had led her to think that he might be gay, though he had ridiculed the idea when she had taxed him with it. Now that their respective families had moved away from Nettleford, they saw each other less frequently but still remained friends. Amanda had been pleased to discover that they were both staying overnight in the same house for the party that saw the start of their troubles.

Amanda's memory of the party afterwards tended to be selective and seen through a haze of red wine. She and Jeremy had been fooling around when the firework display began and she had suggested they should go for a spin in his car. She was in an amorous mood and Jeremy seemed to present her with a renewed challenge.

It was when they were in the car he told her he had taken a firework from the unattended box in the porch of the hall where the party was being held and why didn't they go and wake somebody up with it. It was she who had immediately suggested Oliver Anstey as the victim of their prank. She had disliked him ever since he had shouted at her for failing to keep her dog under control when he was out riding. He had given her a dressing-down that still rankled.

On the way to the Ansteys' house, he had stopped the car at her request and she had asked him to make love to her.

"Not even a contortionist could in this car," he had remarked, which she thought was a feeble excuse, even though she could see the practical difficulties. They had settled for a smooch, which lasted until he said he was getting cold.

When they arrived at the Ansteys', they both got out of the car and she had held the letter box open while he dropped the lighted firework through. At the first police interview, she had readily admitted her part. She had no real regrets, apart from a tinge of remorse for the worry and embarrassment she had caused her parents. Even though they no longer lived in the district, they were still remembered by a lot of local residents and Amanda had certainly left her mark as their headstrong and tearaway daughter.

She had been confident that Uncle Malcolm would get them both off with a fine and the prospect of court proceedings occasioned her no worry.

The surprise came when Uncle Malcolm announced that, after giving the case considerable thought, he was now sure that she was covering up for her co-defendant and that it would be better if they were separately represented and if she assumed the role of an innocent who had been led astray. Though she demurred, he had been insistent and had added that, in any event, he no longer intended representing Jeremy.

"It wouldn't be appropriate," he had said in a tone that brooked no further argument. He had also said it was most important that she had no contact whatsoever with Jeremy as this could be misunderstood and could compromise her defence.

Though mystified by his attitude, she had gone along with his advice for the sake of not further upsetting her parents. When she saw Jeremy at court, she had tried to explain to him what had happened, but he had been in such a state that he didn't seem to take anything in . . . And then that very morning had come the news that Malcolm Palfrey had been found dead in Pan's Place of all unlikely spots. She knew it well as a place for dalliance on a summer's evening. Now she had just heard that Jeremy had confessed to the killing, a telephone call from Madge Seeberg bringing her the news.

For somebody who didn't normally spend a great deal of time reflecting on what lay in the past, she found herself in a state of considerable confusion. Somewhere along the line, something had gone terribly wrong, but she had no idea at what point.

She felt she must do something to help Jeremy. But what?

★ ★ ★

Ever since the discovery of Malcolm Palfrey's body, Tom Berry had begun his morning round of the park by visiting Pan's Place. It was not that he expected to find further dead bodies, but he liked to think he was Rosa's agent looking out for some tiny clue that had escaped everyone's notice.

239

On the day after Jeremy's visit to Nettleford police station, he was startled to find a bunch of flowers resting on the bench where the body had lain. They were freesias in a slender cellophane envelope. He carefully opened the top and sniffed the scent. Then he looked to see if there was a card attached, but there was not.

Somebody had clearly placed them there deliberately, rather in the way that the scene of a tragic accident will attract bunches of flowers in memory of those who died.

He put the freesias back on the bench and pondered on what to do. He had already decided to let Rosa know, the question was whether he should also inform the police. It wasn't that anyone had broken the law by putting them there; nevertheless, it was a gesture that those investigating Malcolm Palfrey's death might regard as significant.

He glanced at his watch. It was only just after eight o'clock and if he hastened to the public call box at the railway station, he should catch Rosa before she left home. There was a steady stream of people crossing the park on their way to London and a new day of work. Though not far short of the winter solstice, it was a reasonably light morning.

Rosa was on the verge of departure when her phone rang, having decided to get to the office early to make up for having been out most of the previous day.

Her heart gave a small lurch when she heard Tom's voice. For one moment she thought he must be in a call box in the vicinity and wanted to pay a breakfast visit, then she heard him say from where he was phoning. In a few crisp sentences he told her of his discovery.

"How extraordinary!" Rosa said when he finished. "I don't know what to make of it."

"Do you think I should inform the police?"

"It can't be wrong to do so," she said uncertainly. "Otherwise, what'll you do with the flowers?"

"Take them home and keep them for you."

Unsure whether he was being serious (he had a way of not signalling his jokes) she said quickly, "I think you should definitely inform the police. Take the flowers with you and say where you found them."

"Who do you think left them there?"

"I haven't a clue. Presumably somebody who has a fond memory of Mr Palfrey.

"Or a guilty conscience perhaps?"

"I'm not with you."

"Someone who may feel that he or she was in some way responsible for his death."

"That doesn't sound very plausible."

"You're probably right. So when am I going to see you again?"

The question came out of the blue and threw Rosa into an immediate dither.

"I don't really know . . . "

"What about this evening?"

"This evening?" she echoed as she tried to get control of her thoughts. "I think I may be tied up with a late conference."

"Then you'll want to relax when you get home."

"Yes, I'll probably have an early night."

"Suits me. Suppose I come along around eight-thirty?"

Rosa knew she ought to say a firm "no" to the proposal, but firmness was the last thing she felt capable of summoning up.

"I'm not sure, Tom — " she said helplessly.

"If you don't want to see me, all you have to do is not open the door. I shan't break down. Meanwhile, I'd better let the police know about these flowers."

He rang off before Rosa could speak again. As she drove to the office, she reflected on their conversation. She knew perfectly well that she wouldn't refuse to open the door to him, so the sensible thing was to suppress her inhibitions and look forward to his visit. But how shamefully embarrassing if Peter Chen phoned when Tom was at the flat. If Peter came home it might break the spell Tom seemed to have cast over her.

When some twelve hours later she went to her front door to let him in, he stood before her clutching a bunch of freesias.

"For you," he said, holding them out. Observing her expression he grinned and went on, "I bought them on my way. The other lot lie withering in Sergeant Whitehead's office."

Rosa relaxed and smiled. "What did the police say?"

"They thanked me, insisted on taking a further statement as to exactly how and where I'd found them, and when I left they were still scratching their heads."

It was after midnight before Tom departed. And Peter Chen hadn't called.

"A most enjoyable evening," he remarked as he kissed her goodnight. "And don't tell me you didn't enjoy it too."

Rosa gave him a misty smile as she went to close the front door.

"You're a very sweet person, she said. "Sweet, but mixed-up."

"Look who's talking!" he replied as he set off down the stairs.

17

ROSA awoke the next morning with a hangover. A moral hangover. Having been brought up in a manse and not exposed to the decadent ways of the outside world until she left her father's rectory in Herefordshire at the age of eighteen to live in London, she supposed her feeling was virtually inevitable. The seeds sown in the course of one's upbringing often bore fruit that lasted the rest of one's life.

In the present instance it was not only that she had slept with a young man outside the bond of marriage that troubled her conscience — after all, that had happened before — as the fact that the young man in question would be a prosecution witness should Jeremy Scott-Pearce ever be charged. Admittedly, Tom's evidence was seemingly uncontroversial, but the fact remained that they would be on opposite sides and Rosa could find herself the target of angry disapprobation if the truth about their relationship were to come out. That was the sharp horn of her dilemma and the crux of her moral hangover. She had behaved unprofessionally, she kept telling herself. Not only that, but she was pretty sure that she would continue to do so if the opportunity arose. There were times when sin had a more than usually seductive appeal.

She was thankful that her father was no longer alive. Right up to the end of his life he had worried about her living in the wicked capital. Her mother had died when Rosa was still a schoolgirl and was now little more than a faded memory.

After spending the greater part of the day in court, Rosa didn't get back to her office until four o'clock.

"Any urgent calls, Steph?" she asked as she came in.

"Mr Scott-Pearce senior has been on the phone approximately once an hour," Stephanie observed drily. "I told him you wouldn't be back till late afternoon, but that hasn't stopped him calling."

"Did he say what he wanted?"

"No, except that it was a matter of great urgency and importance."

"I suppose I'd better call him back."

"No need, he'll be phoning again in a few minutes."

"Presumably it's about his son."

"This could be him now," Stephanie said as she manipulated a switch on the panel in front of her. She gave Rosa a small nod. "It is," she added as Rosa hurried off to her room.

"I've been trying to reach you all day," Charles Scott-Pearce said aggressively, almost before Rosa had the receiver to her ear. "What's all this about Jeremy and the police? He says he's made a statement. Why on earth did you let him do that?"

"He was insistent."

"Why wasn't I informed what was happening?"

"That was up to Jeremy — "

"I thought I could trust you."

"Look, Mr Scott-Pearce, I represent your son, not you — "

"Who do you think is paying the bill?" he broke in.

"That really has nothing to do with

it," Rosa replied. "Your son is over twenty-one and no longer subject to parental control. In law, that is."

"Nevertheless, I'd have expected you to get in touch with me."

Rosa knew that she must keep her cool. Charles Scott-Pearce's annoyance was no more than she had expected, but for all that she didn't enjoy being the target of anyone's recrimination.

"As a matter of fact," she said coldly, "I told Jeremy he ought to talk to you before he took such an irrevocable step, but he said his mind was made up and nothing would alter it. And, in any event, you were travelling in Italy and couldn't be contacted."

There was a hostile silence for several seconds before Charles Scott-Pearce spoke again.

"Perhaps you'd be good enough to tell me what Jeremy said to the police." His tone was stiff and uncompromising.

"I'll do better, I'll read you his statement. I have a copy on my desk." When she finished, she added, "You'll have noticed that Jeremy purports to have no idea why Mr Palfrey wanted to meet him and chose such an improbable venue."

"What is absolutely clear is that Malcolm Palfrey was intending to commit murder and was hoist with his own petard."

"It looks that way."

"It does more than look it."

"Should the police charge Jeremy in respect of Mr Palfrey's death, I think he'll have a very good chance of acquittal. That is, unless the police have a few cards up their sleeve, of which we're unaware at the moment."

There was a further pause before Charles Scott-Pearce said, "Of course the whole statement is nonsense. Surely you realise that?"

"Realise what?"

"That Jeremy's invented the whole thing."

"For what reason?"

"He's covering up for somebody."

"He didn't give me that impression and I questioned him closely before we went down to Nettleford."

"Nevertheless, that's what he's doing, covering up."

"If that's true, the police are going to be extremely angry. He'll be charged with wasting their time by making a false statement."

"Better that than being charged with murder."

"What makes you so certain he's covering up for somebody?"

"I just know."

Rosa sighed. "Incidentally, are you calling from Geneva?"

"Yes."

"Then I think it would be a good thing if you flew over and we sorted the whole thing out."

"Very well, I'll come tomorrow. I have to be in Paris the following day, but perhaps we could meet at Heathrow. I'll get my secretary to book a suite at one of the airport hotels. Will that suit you?"

"I can't manage before four o'clock, as I shall be in court."

"That'll suit me. I'll fly on to Paris afterwards. I'll get my secretary to phone you as soon as she's made the arrangements. Anything else?"

"What about Jeremy, will you let him know?"

"You think he ought to join us?"

"But of course," Rosa said in an astonished tone. It was one of the least satisfactory telephone conversations she had ever had, and now it was touching on the surrealistic. "It's his confession to the police that we have to discuss. If he is covering up for somebody, we've got to find out who — "

"I can tell you that now, Miss Epton."

"Who?"

"Me."

* * *

Charles Scott-Pearce was waiting by the door of his suite when she arrived the next afternoon. She peered past him into the drawing room and saw that it was empty.

"I'm afraid Jeremy couldn't come," he said, reading her gaze aright.

"What sort of game are you playing?" Rosa demanded angrily. "I've trekked out here at considerable inconvenience and apparently to no purpose. I think I ought to tell you that my time comes expensive and that I don't appreciate being led a dance of this sort. My guess is that you've made no attempt to get Jeremy here."

While she spoke, he walked over to the desk and opened a black leather document case which bore the initials 'C S-P' in gold letters. Turning round he said, "Here's a cheque for a thousand pounds on account. If it's not enough, say so and I'll write you another. And here" — he held out an unsealed manila envelope — "is my statement. After we spoke on the phone yesterday I decided it would be better if I came armed with a written statement which you can pass on to the police. It'll also save time. I've got forty minutes before the check-in time for my flight to Paris, so I suggest you read it through and ask me any questions you want before I leave."

The statement which Rosa took from the envelope was typed on sheets of crisp white paper. She glanced at the end and saw that it was dated that day and signed 'Charles Scott-Pearce' in the presence of 'Monique Lescaut' to whom it was dictated and by whom it was typed. Rosa's eyes skimmed over

252

the opening paragraphs until it reached one which began:

A few days before my son and Amanda Ritchie were due to appear in court, Malcolm Palfrey telephoned me in Geneva and said that it was very important that we should meet before the case. As he had annoyed me considerably by throwing over my son's defence, I was in no mood to accommodate him. He said it had to do with a property scheme in which we were involved, which was highly confidential and had to remain that way. However, as I was coming over for my son's court appearance, I reluctantly agreed to meet him and suggested he should come to the hotel in London where I was proposing to stop the night, but he said that wouldn't suit him. I then suggested his office after it had closed, but he said somebody might see us. I then asked him somewhat testily where *he* suggested and he said the corner of the park at Shilman Green known as Pan's Place. He added that absolute secrecy and privacy would be assured if we met there. I thought he was raving mad and told him so. I knew, however, that he'd always been rather keen on cloak and dagger exploits. In the end to avoid further argument I agreed to meet him there at nine-thirty . . . When I arrived he was already there and sprang up from the bench on which he'd been sitting. "It's showdown time, Charles," he said. "You've tried to cheat me once too often." I saw that he was brandishing a pistol . . . I grappled with him . . . the pistol went off and he slumped back on to the seat . . . I realised he was dead . . . I drove straight back to London in the car I had hired and returned to Geneva on the first plane next morning. That was why I never turned up at court for Jeremy's case, though I knew, of course, that it wouldn't go ahead. I told him on the phone what had happened before I flew out. Jeremy is very loyal and a devoted son and must have misguidedly decided to shoulder the responsibility for Palfrey's death. He would feel that I had more to lose than he and that in some tribal way he was making it up to me for the times he had fallen short as a son. I have asked Miss Epton to forward this statement to the police at Nettleford who can contact me at my Geneva address. I'll then let them know when I'll next be in England.

"Is that all right?" he asked, when Rosa looked up.

"More to the point, is it the truth?"

He frowned. "Of course."

"Is it true you've tried to cheat Malcolm Palfrey?"

He gave a small, mirthless laugh. "In fact it was the other way round. On one occasion he failed to disclose an extra ten thousand pounds he'd obtained on one of our transactions and which he was proposing to hang on to. Fortunately, I found out and he paid up without a murmur."

"Does Jeremy know we're having this meeting?"

"No, I'll call him when I get home tomorrow evening. Now that you've read my statement, you can see why there was no point in his being here." He paused and stared at the pages of his statement which Rosa had put down on a table. "I'd like you to post that to the Nettleford police as soon as may be." He glanced once more at his watch. "It's time I got a taxi across to the terminal. I'll keep in touch with you, Miss Epton."

It was apparent to Rosa as she followed him across the hotel lobby that the staff who observed their departure assumed, as a matter of course, that the suite had been booked for one purpose only. They'd have been incredulous to learn that its two occupants hadn't even held hands.

★ ★ ★

Robin and Susan Snaith and their two children lived a few miles west of the airport and Rosa's immediate thought after parting company with Charles Scott-Pearce was that she must talk

256

to Robin. It was just after five o'clock and she knew that he'd be home early as he and Susan were due to attend some local function at seven. The need to talk to him was imperative as she was feeling more confused than at any other time in her professional life.

She went back inside the hotel and found a telephone.

"Hello, Rosa," Susan said as soon as she heard the familiar voice. "If you want Robin, I'm afraid he's not back yet, but I'm expecting him any minute. Where are you speaking from?"

"I'm at one of the airport hotels and I'd like to see Robin as soon as I can. May I come along?"

"Of course. We're not going out till seven and Robin doesn't need more than ten minutes to change. It's a charity dinner and dance. Each year we say we won't go again, but then we have our arms twisted and give in. It's not even one of those functions that turns out better than you expect. Anyway, see you in a few minutes."

As Rosa parked in their drive, a plane skimmed overhead, seemingly little more than rooftop high. For a few seconds it blotted out everything else. Robin had been born in the house and grown up in what had then been a rural ambience. Fortunately, he and Susan had grown accustomed to the dosage of noise that drove their visitors to near madness.

"Come in," Susan said, greeting Rosa at the door. "He really should be here any minute." She gave her visitor a quick glance. "Nothing wrong, is there? I mean, you're all right?"

"For the first time in years, Susan, I feel out of my depth, but I'm sure Robin'll know what to do."

"Is it something to do with your Nettleford case?"

"Yes. Has Robin talked about it?"

"Only to say you were dealing with a lot of troublesome people and that some wily solicitor had inveigled you into taking on the case."

"Inveigled is certainly the right word. Did Robin mention that the solicitor in question met a sudden end?"

"Yes, and I read about it in the paper. Let's go into the kitchen and have a cuppa. Or you can have something stronger if you wish."

"No, a cup of tea sounds perfect."

As she led the way down a long passage to the enormous, refurbished kitchen at the rear of the house, Susan went on, "Everything's unusually peaceful as the children are stopping the night with friends. We shan't see them again until they come home from school tomorrow."

A few minutes later a distant door opened and closed and approaching footsteps heralded Robin's arrival.

"Hello, Rosa," he said genially. "I saw your car outside."

"Rosa has a problem to discuss with you," Susan said, after giving her husband a kiss. "I'll go and change while you two talk."

"Don't I even get a cup of tea?" he enquired plaintively.

His wife poured one and put it on the table in front of him. Then giving his head a friendly pat, she turned and left.

"I take it your problem has something to do with Scott-Pearce senior?"

Rosa nodded and pulled the statement from her bag. "Read this, Robin."

She watched him intently while he did

so. When he reached the end, he looked up and met her gaze.

"I don't believe a word of it," he said. "Who ever heard of two professional men holding a business meeting in a dark corner of a park reserved for youthful copulation? It's too absurd for words."

"Don't forget it was Malcolm Palfrey who chose the site and that he had in mind an execution rather than a business discussion."

"I don't pretend to know what Palfrey was up to, but I'm darned certain he never lured Charles Scott-Pearce to Pan's Place on the pretext given in this statement."

"What about Jeremy?"

"It's slightly less implausible in his case, but still some distance from reality. Father's and son's statements are virtually the same when it comes to what happened. It's clear that their intention is to muddy the waters and confuse the police. With luck, they'll both live to regret it."

"What am I to do, Robin?"

"Ring Harshaw tomorrow morning and tell him everything and say that you're forwarding this statement as requested. Make it clear that you're not acting as Charles Scott-Pearce's legal adviser, but simply as a post office." He paused. "There's only one bit I'd be inclined to leave out, namely that Scott-Pearce told you on the phone his son was covering up for him. Let Harshaw assume that the written statement was your first indication of that." Observing Rosa's unhappy expression, he added, "That's all you can do. No more, no less."

18

EACH Sunday when Madge Seeberg talked to her sister on the telephone, their somewhat one-sided conversation would end with Doll exhorting her to take care and not do anything foolhardy. She was ever reminding Madge how their father used to refer to her as lion-hearted and how she, Doll, wouldn't say 'boo' to a goose.

If Madge had given heed to her sister's admonition, she would almost certainly have stayed alive and not met death in the self-same spot as her employer.

Since Malcolm Palfrey's demise, her one thought had been to protect his memory.

It had been while she was conducting a final clear-out of his desk that she came upon a letter hidden at the back of a drawer. Its presence puzzled her, particularly as it didn't appear to have been opened. Closer examination, however, revealed that it was only partially sealed. It gave the appearance of having been steamed open and stuck down again. Miss Seeberg popped it into her handbag to take home with her. As she left Mr Palfrey's room she bumped into Mr Chance who asked her coldly what she was doing.

"I'm still going through Mr Palfrey's drawers," she had replied with equal chill.

"Well, please don't remove anything without first speaking to me."

You'll be lucky, she thought contemptuously as she walked away.

When she got home that evening she took the letter from her handbag and gave the envelope a hard stare. She was in no doubt about whose handwriting it was. She even remembered its arrival a day or two before Mr Palfrey's death. It had been her custom to open what was plainly his official mail, but to leave anything that looked private or personal unopened on his desk. This letter came into that category. Subsequently, he never made any reference to it and, to be perfectly frank, she forgot all about it. It wasn't as if it had aroused her curiosity in any way. Hence her surprise at finding it tucked away out of sight at the back of one of his drawers. The police had made a cursory search of his office, but had not found anything of significance.

With the aid of a steaming kettle, she now opened the envelope and extracted the single folded sheet of paper. It was a short letter, but even as she read its few sentences, she realised she was within reach of understanding how Mr Palfrey came to die. She had always known the 'how' and now she knew the 'wherefore', though the 'why' still remained in the realm of speculation.

If she had been as circumspect as her sister, Dolly, she would immediately have gone to the police with her find.

But foolhardiness is apt to be contemptuous of convention and Madge found herself fired with a determination to dig out the final segment of truth relating to her employer's death.

It was a few days later that Tom Berry, on his early morning round of the park, found her body in Pan's Place. She appeared to have been strangled with her own silk head scarf A bunch of freesias lay on the ground beside her.

The discovery of a second body in Pan's Place shook Tom much more than had the first. His hospital experience had accustomed him to dead bodies, but there was something infinitely pathetic about Madge Seeberg's crumpled shape. Though, at the time, he didn't know who she was, he was quite sure she must be connected with the Palfrey case. He assumed she was the person who had brought the earlier bunch of freesias he had found at the site.

He emerged through the bushes that guarded Pan's Place and stared about the park. There was a steady stream of commuters hurrying in the direction of the station to catch their train to London, but he ruled out the idea of waylaying one and enlisting his help. The real danger was from children going in the opposite direction on their way to school, but it would be a further half-hour before that particular contra-flow began.

Returning through the gap in the bushes while he considered what to do, he bent down and lightly touched

Madge Seeberg's cheek. It was as cold as frozen marble. He reckoned she must have lain there all night.

Leaving the scene again, he decided to block the entrance with his wheelbarrow and hope that it would deter anyone from entering. Then he set off across the park at a trot, making for the public call box at Shilman Green railway station.

His first call was to the Nettleford police. Declaring his identity, he said he had just found the body of a dead woman in Pan's Place.

"You're quite sure about that?" asked a disbelieving voice.

"Absolutely sure."

"If this is a hoax — "

"It's not a hoax and if you don't get somebody here quickly, you're going to have something worse than egg on your face."

"OK, wait till we come."

Tom reckoned it would be ten or fifteen minutes at least before the police arrived. That would give him time to call Rosa.

On this occasion she was nibbling at a slice of toast and honey and glancing at the paper's headlines when the phone rang.

"It's me again," said the now familiar voice. "I've just found another body in Pan's Place . . . "

When he had finished, Rosa said in a shocked voice, "Its sounds like Miss Seeberg. She was Malcolm Palfrey's secretary."

"That figures. Would she have been likely to lay flowers on the spot where he died?"

"Yes. In fact, I immediately thought of her when you found the first lot. You think she was strangled?"

"I don't think, I know. Why don't you drive down?"

"Because the police would wonder what I was doing. They'd be immediately suspicious."

"Then I'll come and see you this evening and give you a full report on the day's events."

"Yes, all right," Rosa said uncertainly.

"I'd better ring off now. I've just seen a police car turn into Station Road. Expect me between eight and nine."

With Madge Seeberg's death, Chief Inspector Harshaw felt that at last the ice had cracked and things would move toward a conclusion. It was a clinical way of viewing the events of Pan's Place, but it gave Harshaw a charge of fresh energy and helped to mitigate the frustration he had been experiencing since receiving Charles Scott-Pearce's statement. A call to Rosa, followed by two to Geneva had merely exacerbated his sense of frustration. To have statements from two different people (albeit father and son) each confessing to causing Malcolm Palfrey's death in circumstances of self-defence was a crazy situation and he found himself secretly agreeing with Sergeant Whitehead that they should both be locked up and held incommunicado until the truth came out. Unfortunately, the law didn't provide for such practical action.

Charles Scott-Pearce had said he expected to be in England later in the month or at the beginning of January and would let Harshaw know as soon as his arrangements were made. Meanwhile, Jeremy was due to answer to his police bail in a week's time. Harshaw didn't pretend to know which of them, if either, was telling the truth, but was determined that they should pay for any proven manipulation of the administration of justice.

When he arrived at Pan's Place shortly after nine o'clock that morning, one swift look was enough to tell him that the dead woman was, indeed, Madge Seeberg and that she had been cruelly murdered. Even if her features had not been identifiable, he would have recognised the mauve chiffon scarf that was wound tightly round her neck. She had a number of scarves of that colour, which Harshaw over the years had come to associate with her.

One of the local doctors, whose services the police frequently used, was in attendance.

"I'd say she's been dead between twelve and fifteen hours," he said, "and that death was due to strangulation by a ligature. It looks as if the scarf was pulled tight from behind." He straightened up.

"Whoever performs the post mortem will be able to fill in the details." He paused. "She was Malcolm Palfrey's secretary, wasn't she?"

"Yes."

"Poor soul! Presumably their two deaths are connected. Well, I'd better return to my morning surgery and prescribe for the more common ills of headaches and mysterious rashes."

Within the next half-hour Madge Seeberg's body was moved to the mortuary for an autopsy and a team of officers moved in on the scene in a search for clues.

Harshaw was about to leave when Colin Tearcey, the Assistant Chief Constable, appeared.

"Thought I'd find you here," he remarked as he looked about him with an inquisitive gaze. "By the way, who's the young chap the other side of the bushes?"

"His name's Berry. He's the park-keeper."

"Wasn't it he who discovered Palfrey's body?"

"Yes. This one, too."

"Doesn't that put him under suspicion?"

Harshaw shook his head. "I've told him he better not find a third or he could find himself in trouble. He's a bright young chap and he'll make a good witness when we get to court."

"When! So what's your next move, Richard?"

"I want to find out the exact movements of a number of people between six and ten o'clock yesterday evening. The Scott-Pearces for a start, also Adrian Chance and Mrs Palfrey. I'll make a plea for anyone who was in the area between those hours to come forward. And I'll find out if the cars owned by any of those people happened to be seen."

"You think Miss Seeberg's murderer is one of those four?"

Harshaw nodded. "I'll even narrow it, sir, and say it was either Scott-Pearce or his son."

"On the strength of their admissions to date?"

"Yes." In a grim tone he added, "Whoever killed Miss Seeberg won't be able to claim he did so in self-defence."

"I seem to recall," the Assistant Chief Constable remarked, "that she herself was sure that Adrian Chance murdered Palfrey."

"That's correct, sir. It's why I want to check his movements as well as the others."

"And Mrs Palfrey? What makes you think it could be her?"

Harshaw pulled a face. "I'm certain she's hiding something, sir. I have been all along. I wish I knew what."

"I wonder what it was Miss Seeberg found out that made her a threat to the person who murdered her?"

"If we knew that, sir, we'd know everything."

★ ★ ★

Rosa realised that she should call Jeremy and warn him that the police would almost certainly be getting in touch with him sooner rather than later. It was not, however, a prospect she welcomed as she had come to regard any dealings with her client as being similar to a walk across quicksands.

Tom had phoned again almost as soon as she reached the office to confirm that the dead person was, indeed, Madge Seeberg and that it was estimated she had died between six and ten the previous evening.

It would normally have been a logical conclusion that the same person had killed both Malcolm Palfrey and his secretary. But if this were Jeremy and the first killing had been in self-defence as he asserted, what reason could there have been for the second? It was at this point that logic seemed to break down . . .

As long as Jeremy remained her client, she owed him a duty. It was with this thought uppermost in her mind that she put through a call soon after Tom had phoned again.

The phone rang unanswered for a long time and she was about to put the receiver down when a sleepy voice came on the line.

"Jeremy?"

"Yes, who's that?"

"It's Rosa Epton."

"Oh, hello. Is it about my father?

273

I gather you met him at the airport and he told you it was he who shot Malcolm — "

"I'm not calling about your father," Rosa broke in. Indeed, the father-son dispute was the last matter in which she wished to embroil herself at that moment. "I'm phoning to tell you that Miss Seeberg has been found murdered and the police are certain to want to question you." The silence that ensued became such that Rosa wondered if they had been cut off. "Are you still there?"

"Yes."

"And you heard what I said."

"About Miss Seeberg? Yes. So you're telling me I'm an automatic suspect?" His tone was querulous.

"What I'm telling you," Rosa said firmly, "is that the police will wish to question you about your movements yesterday evening. I'm not suggesting you'll be the only person."

"Around what time yesterday evening?"

"Between six and ten. Where were you then?"

"Here at the flat."

"Can anyone confirm that?"

"I shouldn't think so," he said with a touch of bravado.

"My mother's away for a couple of days and I'm on my own."

"Did you talk to anyone on the phone in the course of the evening?"

"No. I had a headache and went to bed early. I didn't want to be disturbed so I unplugged the phone. I didn't reconnect it until about an hour ago." He paused. "Why should anyone want to kill Miss Seeberg? I wouldn't have thought she ever did anybody any harm." He fell silent again, then said, "I shall refuse to talk to the police unless you're present. So that shit Whitehead can go and stuff himself."

"I think you should be ready for the police to question you more strenuously than before."

"They can shake me till I rattle, but I'll still not confess to something I've not done."

After their conversation was concluded, Rosa sat for a while staring at her desk. It struck her as curious that Jeremy had neither asked how Madge Seeberg came by her death, nor where.

* * *

Chief Inspector Harshaw was not as far forward with his enquiry at the end of the day as he had hoped to be.

He had reached the conclusion that Madge Seeberg was on a second mission to lay flowers at the site of her employer's death when she met her end. Though it struck him as a bizarre thing to do, it was perhaps understandable on the part of a devoted secretary who had probably harboured a secret passion towards her employer.

But if that much was reasonably clear, nothing else was and he was still in the dark as to who had followed her to Pan's Place and strangled her. Or why.

He had hoped for a quick lead that would enable him to charge Jeremy Scott-Pearce, but it was a hope not fulfilled. Rosa had driven her client down to Nettleford in the afternoon and they had spent forty-five minutes at the station. She had offered to bring Jeremy as soon as Harshaw got in touch with her. But Jeremy had been unshakeable in his denial of any involvement in the murder and Harshaw was without the necessary ammunition. His chagrin had been increased when independent evidence was forthcoming that Jeremy's car had remained outside the block of flats the whole evening. This was confirmed by an indignant neighbour who liked to park his own car in that particular slot.

He had also drawn a blank with Nadine Palfrey whose presence at home the whole evening had been confirmed by the Italian au pair and by her two daughters. WPC Perkins had been helpful in eliciting this information in a tactful manner.

Before Rosa and Jeremy reached the police station, Harshaw had spent over an hour at the office of Palfrey and Co. where Madge Seeberg's violent death had cast a pall of shock and fear. Adrian Chance affected to have no idea who might have killed her, though it seemed to Harshaw he was a distinctly worried man. He said he had been at home the whole evening, whither he had gone straight from the office around six-thirty and he had not left the house till the next morning.

"I take it your wife will be able to confirm that, Mr Chance," Harshaw had said.

Chance had looked taken aback and embarrassed. "She's away. She had to go up to Derbyshire to visit her mother who's sick."

"Is there anyone who can confirm you didn't leave the house yesterday evening?"

"Really, Chief Inspector," Chance said in a blustering tone, "I hope you don't seriously think I killed the unfortunate woman."

"It's no more than a routine enquiry," Harshaw said pacifically, at the same time wondering why the solicitor was being so prickly. Then he remembered that Adrian Chance was known for reacting like a porcupine under attack.

Of the other members of staff he had interviewed, Austin Fulwood, the outdoor clerk, was the most willing to talk.

"She was closer to Palfrey than anyone," he remarked with a knowing expression.

"What's that meant to mean?"

"That she was more than just a secretary."

"Are you telling me she was his mistress?"

"She'd like to have been all right. Poor old Madge! She'd have done anything for Mr Palfrey."

"So she wasn't his mistress?" Harshaw said a trifle impatiently.

"That didn't mean she didn't know more about him than anyone else in the office. She wasn't his confidential secretary all those years without discovering a few of his secrets."

"Do you think that was why she was killed?"

Austin Fulwood nodded sagely. He had never been one averse to voicing his views. "That's where you'll find the solution, Chief Inspector. Dig into her relationship with Mr Palfrey." He gave Harshaw another knowing look. "If Madge could speak from the grave, I know who she would tell you had murdered her."

"She's not yet in her grave," Harshaw said irritably.

"Anyway, Mr Chance never left home

yesterday evening."

He had known Austin Fulwood a long time and regarded him as a tiresome windbag. The police, of course, gleaned information wherever they could and tiresome windbags were often a useful source. Harshaw, however, felt reasonably sure that in this instance the firm's outdoor clerk was merely feeding his own sense of self-importance.

It was nearly midnight before Harshaw decided there was nothing further to be done that day and he ought to go home and snatch some sleep while he could. As he passed through the general office, a uniformed PC was just leaving the station to go on duty. Harshaw gave him a weary smile.

"How's the enquiry going, sir?" the officer asked. Then before Harshaw could reply, he went on, "I understand you were enquiring if anyone saw Mr Adrian Chance's car yesterday evening — "

"Among others, yes."

"Well, I did, sir. Around eight o'clock."

"Are you sure it was Mr Chance's car?"

"Yes, sir. I once had occasion to book

him for parking on a double yellow line, so I know it."

"Who was driving?"

"Mr Chance, sir," the PC said in faint surprise at the question.

"You're sure of that, too?"

"Yes."

"Which direction was he going?"

"He turned down Gillam Avenue."

"Did he now!" Harshaw exclaimed with sudden interest, as he recalled that 16 Gillam Avenue was Madge Seeberg's home.

★ ★ ★

Tom Berry lay on his back in front of the fire in Rosa's living room. He had just had a bath and a towel was wrapped round his waist. His still wet hair was slicked back and Rosa thought how absurdly young and innocent he looked as she observed him from the settee where she was sitting with her legs tucked beneath her. It showed how misleading appearances could be, she reflected. Young he might be, but innocent, never.

He raised an arm and took one of her

hands, which he gently caressed.

"You're in a mess, aren't you?" he said. "I mean, having a client whom you neither like nor trust."

"It's happened before."

"But this Scott-Pearce youth isn't merely untrustworthy, he's manipulating you."

Rosa nodded slowly. "That's what really annoys me."

"At least, you'll mind less if he turns out to be guilty."

"I dislike having the truth deliberately withheld from me. I don't expect all my clients to be innocent, because most of them aren't. But it's the feeling that I'm being manipulated that really gets me."

"When I found that poor old girl dead this morning, my immediate thought was, I hope they catch the bastard that did it. I didn't feel that way when I discovered Palfrey's body."

Rosa sighed. "Well, there's nothing I can do until the police make a move. Assuming that somebody other than Jeremy Scott-Pearce is charged with Miss Seeberg's murder, there's still going to be a lot of clearing up where he's concerned. There's the outstanding criminal damage offence, not to mention his statement about Malcolm Palfrey's death. It's all going to take quite a lot of sorting out."

"It seems he'll need your services for some time to come."

"I'm afraid so."

"I wonder what I can do to help," he said in a thoughtful voice.

"You've helped a lot already."

"Helped *and* embarrassed." He gave her a small smile that had a tinge of sadness about it. "Oh, I'm aware how you feel about my being a police witness and all that, and the last thing I'd want is to make things awkward for you."

"We must keep our fingers crossed. And if we do find ourselves in court on opposite sides of the fence, we'll have to tread carefully."

"Don't worry, I shan't suddenly proclaim undying love for you from the witness box. But to return to what I was saying, I wonder if I couldn't help further . . . "

"How?"

"Mrs Palfrey is still advertising for a part-time gardener. There's a card in one of the newsagent's windows. Why don't I apply? After all, Saturdays and Sundays are my own."

Rosa frowned. "You'd be running a risk."

"What risk?"

"I'm not sure, but I know the police wouldn't approve."

"Who cares!"

"And Mrs Palfrey might think you were up to something."

"All the better."

"And, anyway, what do you expect to find out?" Rosa asked, feeling that her defences were being eroded.

"It's my hunch that the motive for everything that's happened lies hidden there."

Rosa gave him an anxious glance.

"For heaven's sake, Tom, don't go breaking the law."

He jumped up from the floor and put his arms around her.

"Have confidence in me. My psychiatrist said I must build up my confidence and you can help."

He gave Rosa one of his unfathomable looks, so that she didn't know whether to laugh or to make soothing sounds. She didn't do either and it was several hours before he left for home.

19

HARSHAW was on Adrian Chance's doorstep shortly before eight o'clock the next morning. The solicitor appeared startled when he saw who his early morning visitor was.

"I'm having breakfast," he said, in the hope perhaps that this might have the effect of sending Harshaw on his way.

"That's all right. I can talk to you while you eat."

Chance turned with obvious reluctance, leaving the officer to close the front door and follow him to the kitchen. There was a half-eaten bowlful of cereal on the table, together with two slices of toast, a jar of marmalade and a carton of butter spread; also a mug of tea. As he gazed at the table, Harshaw reflected that it was more than he ate even when he had time for breakfast.

The solicitor sat down and, pushing

the bowl of cereal to one side, took a slice of toast.

"Well?" he said. "What brings you here at this early hour?"

"I'd have thought you'd guess."

"I dislike guessing games, especially at breakfast," he said coldly.

"You lied to me about your movements the evening before last. I'd like to know why."

Chance paused in the act of buttering a piece of toast.

"I don't think I know what you're talking about," he said.

"You told me that you never left your house between the time you got home from the office around six-thirty and when you set out again the next morning." Chance bit carefully into the piece of toast, but otherwise showed no reaction. "That's what you told me, wasn't it?"

"Something to that effect, I believe."

"It was more than that. It was an unequivocal statement of fact."

Chance shrugged. "I don't have a record of my exact words."

"Well, I do, just as I'm recording this

interview, and I'd like to know why you lied to me on such a serious matter."

"I'm still not clear in what way I'm supposed to have lied to you."

"You were seen driving your car in Nettleford around eight o'clock that evening."

The solicitor slowly laid down his piece of toast.

"Yes, I did go out for a short time," he said at length. "But I assure you there was nothing sinister about it."

"So why did you lie?"

"Because quite frankly I didn't see it as any of your business."

"Would you care to tell me where you went?"

Chance chewed his lower lip in a worried way before replying.

"To see a friend."

"A lady friend?"

Chance nodded. "Don't ask me her name because I shan't tell you!"

Harshaw became thoughtful as he decided whether the moment had come to play his trump card. Perhaps not quite yet. "If she's an innocent party, I have no wish to involve her, but it's up to you to satisfy me on that point."

"You must take my word for it."

"You seem to overlook the fact that it's because I can't take your word I'm here this morning."

The solicitor flushed and glared at his half-eaten slice of toast.

"Anyway," he said suddenly, "it wouldn't be fair to give her name as she wasn't in. I called at her house on spec and she wasn't there."

"Have you spoken to her since?"

"No."

"Well, if she was unaware of your visit, it can't do any harm to tell me the name of the road in which she lives. That won't compromise her."

Chance frowned. "It's a road off London Road," he said.

Liar, Harshaw reflected equably.

"And you drove there straight from home?" he asked.

"Yes."

"Rang the doorbell, got no answer, and drove home again?"

"Precisely."

"So your journey wouldn't have taken you anywhere near Gillam Avenue?"

Chance reacted as if he'd been punched in the solar plexus.

"Gillam Avenue? I don't think I know where that is."

"You know perfectly well where it is. It's where Miss Seeberg lives. Or rather where she used to live."

"I . . . I have no reason to know where she lived," he said desperately.

"You were seen turning into Gillam Avenue around eight o'clock the evening before last."

"Somebody's mistaken."

"Nobody's mistaken. The officer who saw you knows you and your car."

Chance sprang up from his chair and paced up and down the kitchen in an agitated manner.

"All right," he said in an anguished voice. "I did go to see Miss Seeberg, but she wasn't at home."

"Why didn't you tell me that in the first place?"

"Because I knew she was dead and I was scared you'd draw a wrong conclusion. It seemed better to tell a white lie."

"I don't know about its colour, but

it was a thumping great lie," Harshaw remarked.

"You must believe me, Chief Inspector, I didn't kill Miss Seeberg. I give you my word that she wasn't at home and that her bungalow was in darkness."

"Why did you wish to see her?"

"I was sure she knew things about Palfrey's death that she hadn't told anyone. I couldn't talk to her privately in the office, so I decided to visit her at home."

"Why not phone first?"

"A surprise visit seemed better." He paused and went on, "I found her in Palfrey's office a few days ago. She was going through his desk drawers, which she'd already done once, and I had this feeling she was concealing something to do with his death."

"Or was it that you thought she might have discovered something to your detriment?"

"That's absurd."

"And having confirmed your suspicion, you murdered her."

"No."

"You followed her to Shilman Green.

Maybe you even gave her a lift there in your car. That's the reality, isn't it, Mr Chance?"

"It's an outrageous suggestion," Mr Chance spluttered.

"I should now like you to accompany me to the police station where we'll continue this interview."

"But I'm due in the . . . my secretary will wonder what's happened."

"You can call her from the station."

"I'd sooner the office didn't know where I was."

As Harshaw observed the worried and considerably chastened figure in front of him he felt like adding, "And while you're at it, you'd better get yourself a good lawyer."

★ ★ ★

Police stations are functional institutions which provide little incentive to linger within their confines. Those who are given no choice in the matter receive small comfort for their anxious spirits apart from cups of tea.

During the years he had been a

practising solicitor in Nettleford, Adrian Chance had visited the police station on numerous occasions, though this was the first time he was what might be called an involuntary visitor and he found himself viewing his surroundings through very different eyes as he sat alone in Harshaw's office. The Chief Inspector had been waylaid as they entered the station and Chance was waiting with as much enthusiasm as if he were waiting to see the dentist.

Harshaw, meanwhile, had gone along to Sergeant Whitehead's room to meet Joe Mullin, a local cab driver who had come to give the police some information. He and Whitehead appeared to be old friends.

"Tell the Chief Inspector, Joe, what you've just told me," Whitehead said, as he lit one of his cheap, malodorous cigars.

"It's about this old girl who was strangled in the park at Shilman Green. It was me who drove her there. I took the wife up to town yesterday and we didn't get back till late or I'd have come in before. It was the evening before last,

293

I was on the rank at the railway station when I got this call to go to 16 Gillam Avenue to pick up a Miss Seeberg and take her to Shilman Green. No big deal, an easy run and a small tip, I thought to myself — "

"What time did you pick her up?"

"About ten minutes before eight, I'd say. She was ready and came out of the bungalow as soon as I pulled up outside. I asked her where to in Shilman Green and she said she'd like to be dropped at the entrance to the park."

"Did you notice whether she was carrying anything?"

"Yeah, she had this small bunch of flowers."

"Freesias?"

"Search me, guv! I can't tell a gardenia from a geranium."

"Had you ever driven her before?"

"No, though I felt her face was familiar. I now realise I must have seen her about town. I gather she worked at Palfrey's who happen to be my solicitors. That is, when I can't avoid going to a lawyer."

"Did she talk while she was in the cab?"

"No. I made a couple of attempts at conversation, but she obviously didn't want to talk, so I left it at that."

"She didn't ask you to wait for her at the other end?"

"No. She just paid me the fare, added a twenty pence tip and walked off."

"Which direction?"

"Into the park."

"When you picked her up, did you notice any other car in the vicinity?"

"They're parked on both sides in Gillam Avenue."

"Of course. Did you see anybody hanging around?"

Mullin shook his head. "Nope."

"And when you reached Shilman Green, did you observe whether anybody followed her into the park?"

"As a matter of fact, I did. Mind you, I can't say he was following her, but he entered the park just behind her. I caught him briefly in my headlights as I turned the car in the road."

"Can you describe him?"

"Not a hope. All I saw was his back. He was wearing a dark coloured anorak."

"A hat?"

"No hat," Mullin said after a second's pause.

"What sort of age?"

"Could have been anything between twenty and fifty."

Harshaw sighed. Could have been almost anyone. Even a woman in trousers.

"Well, thanks for your help, Joe. Let us know if you happen to recall anything further."

"Will do."

Leaving Sergeant Whitehead to see the cab driver off the premises, Harshaw walked along the corridor to his own office deep in thought. It was useful to have established how Madge Seeberg had got to the scene of her murder, even if it gave no indication as to who had killed her. The person who had entered the park behind her might have had nothing at all to do with her death. For all the police knew, the murderer might have arrived first and been waiting for her. At least it seemed a safe conclusion that they knew one another and had most probably been in touch recently. Otherwise, how would her murderer have known her movements? He wondered how she had been proposing to get home? Perhaps she had been relying on a lift from . . . From whom? Her murderer?

Adrian Chance looked up with a mixture of expectation and defiance as Harshaw came into the room.

"Sorry to have kept you waiting, Mr Chance."

"I'm sure there's nothing further I can tell you, Chief Inspector and I do have a very full day ahead of me."

"There's certainly one thing you can tell me, do you own an anorak?"

"What on earth has that got to do with anything?"

"Do you or don't you?"

"As a matter of fact, I do."

"Were you wearing it on the evening you went to see Miss Seeberg?"

"I really don't remember."

"You must remember."

"What if I was?"

"I'd like to have it for examination."

"This is preposterous."

"We can go and pick it up now. After which you're free to start your busy day in the office."

Chance glared angrily. "You're being very high-handed. I just hope you know what you're doing."

"I certainly hope so, too, Mr Chance."

★ ★ ★

That same morning Tom called Nadine Palfrey to say he had seen her advertisement for a gardener and was the post still vacant?

She sounded curiously hesitant on the phone, but agreed he should come for an interview the next day, which was a Saturday. Twelve noon was the appointed hour and he arrived a few minutes early.

Nadine herself opened the door and led the way into a small front room which she referred to as the television room. Tom had put on a clean pair of jeans for the occasion and was wearing a plaid shirt and a black crew-neck sweater. He had scrubbed the soles of his sneakers so as not to shed lumps of earth inside the house.

"You're younger than I'd expected, Mr Berry," she said as she sat down and indicated that he should do likewise. "Did you say on the phone that you had experience as a park-keeper?"

"Yes, but I'm free on Saturdays and Sundays and . . . well, I need the extra money."

"Are you still employed as a park-keeper?"

"Yes."

"Where?"

"Shilman Green," he said without hesitation. He had known all along there was no way he could duck this question. He went on, "I hope the fact it has sad memories for you won't affect your giving me the job if I'm otherwise suitable."

"I thought your name was familiar," she said in a musing tone. "So it was you who found my husband's body?"

"Yes."

"Is it morbid curiosity that's brought you here?" Her voice had a bitter edge.

"No, nothing like that at all. As I explained, I need to earn some extra money."

"But the card has been in the newsagent's window for weeks. What's made you apply now?"

"The need for money has become more pressing," he said with a deprecating smile. "I want to change my car and it's time to start saving for next year's holiday."

"I take it you have references?"

"Not with me, but I can supply them."

She gave him a sudden, suspicious look. "Did the police suggest you should apply for the job?"

"Good gracious, no," Tom said in surprise.

"You're not a sort of fifth column?"

"Do I look like one?"

She gave a shrug. "It just strikes me as odd your turning up like this."

"If you don't think I'm suitable for the job, Mrs Palfrey, say so and I won't waste any more of our time." He made to get up, but she motioned him to remain seated.

"Did you know my husband?"

"I never met him."

"What about his partner, Mr Chance?"

"I've never met him either." He paused. "It was simply my lot to find your husband's body and that of Miss

Seeberg. I don't wish to sound callous, but it's the same if I find anything lying about in the park, I have to deal with it."

Nadine leaned forward. "Have the police taken you into their confidence?"

He shook his head. "No earthly reason why they should."

"You seem a very articulate park-keeper. Do you hold a diploma of some sort?"

"I was once a medical student . . ."

"What on earth's a medical student doing as a parkkeeper and applying for a jobbing gardener's post?"

"One day, if I get the job and I happen to be in the right mood, I might tell you, Mrs Palfrey. So what about it?"

There was a sudden explosion of noise in the hall and the door was flung open. A girl stood glaring at them.

"How on earth am I supposed to know what to pack if you won't say how long we're going to be away?" she demanded angrily.

"Please go back to your room, Teresa," Nadine Palfrey said in an icy tone. "Can't you see I'm busy? I'll come and help you as soon as I'm free."

The girl glowered first at her mother and then at Tom. She seemed about to give further vent to her feelings, but turned abruptly and departed, slamming the door behind her.

Looking distinctly upset by the intrusion, Nadine Palfrey stood up and walked over to the door.

"Thank you for coming, Mr Berry," she said in a taut voice. "I'll get in touch with you when I've reached a decision."

As Tom drove away, he was more than ever certain that Kingsmere Farm was a Pandora's box of hidden secrets. Teresa Palfrey's interruption had been a cause for astonishment, while her mother's reaction to the outburst had been no less intriguing.

20

ROSA hadn't long returned to the office on Monday after a long morning in court when Robin came in flourishing a newspaper.

"Seen this?" he asked, passing her the paper which was folded at the births and deaths column.

"I haven't had time to glance at more than the headlines," Rosa replied, taking the paper from him. "Where do you want me to look?"

"Deaths, under P."

Rosa let her eye travel down the column. It came to P and stopped.

"Palfrey," she read, 'peacefully at his home near Shrewsbury, Sir Clement Bt, aged 86. Funeral private. No flowers. Donations if desired to the National Trust'.

"Well, well!" she observed thoughtfully. "Is there a longer obituary?"

"No. I don't suppose that an aged baronet rates one unless he has additional achievements to his name."

"So baby Crispin is now Sir Crispin. Sounds like a character in a Victorian melodrama." After a pause, she went on, "How his father would have loved to have been Sir Malcolm! He'd have felt he was Emperor of Nettleford."

"I hope the new baronet won't find his title an embarrassment in this egalitarian age. The prefix 'Sir' always seems to me to give a name a particularly pretentious ring."

"'Donations, if desired, to the National Trust'," Rosa read out. "What can we deduce from that?"

"That the old boy was more interested in preserving our heritage than its inheritors."

After Robin had left her room Rosa read the notice again. Tom had called her on Saturday evening to report on his interview with Nadine Palfrey, in the course of which he mentioned the curious note on which it had ended.

He had suggested he should drive up to town and see her on Sunday, but Rosa had arranged to spend the day with friends who lived near St Albans.

Vicky French was a friend from student times. She was now married to a vet and their home resembled a zoo, in that one could never be sure which of God's creatures would confront one round the next corner. Fortunately their small daughter, Rebecca, mixed happily with all her four-legged companions.

But Tom had been miffed when she said she couldn't cancel her arrangement and she felt obliged to remind him gently that she had had an existence before she ever met him. He became mollified when she agreed to see him one evening the following week. Secretly she hoped it might even be two evenings.

It now seemed to Rosa that Nadine Palfrey's somewhat strained behaviour, as reported by Tom, could be explained by Sir Clement's death. According to the date in the announcement, he had died the previous Thursday, which was two days before Tom had his interview. It could also explain Teresa's angry outburst. The whole family was going up to Shrewsbury for the funeral and probably staying for an indefinite period while things were sorted out. For all

Rosa knew, Sir Clement had owned a stately home which would now, be part of Crispin's inheritance. She could see that his death would produce a great many matters requiring attention. Children are notoriously conservative and Teresa was in rebellious mood at the prospect of being uprooted from her home.

She reached for her copy of Whitaker's Almanack and turned to the section headed 'Baronetage and Knightage'. It occupied thirty pages with three columns of names on each page. There seemed to be an utter profusion of 'Sirs'. Amongst those under the letter 'P' she read 'Sir Clement Ernest Palfrey, Bt (1805)'. Nothing *nouveau riche* about the Palfreys, she reflected, their title was almost two hundred years old. It explained why Malcolm Palfrey had been so anxious to have an heir. He would have regarded it as a tragedy if he had been unable to pass on the title. It was ironic that it had leap-frogged him.

It was on Thursday of the present week that Jeremy was due to answer to his police bail and Rosa decided she ought to remind him of his commitment and discuss travel arrangements. That is to say, whether he would get to Nettleford under his own steam or accept a lift from her. No way would she be a passenger in his car. When she called the Tite Street number, however, there was no answer. Three o'clock in the afternoon wasn't usually a good time to catch young people at home. And as for Mrs Scott-Pearce, she always seemed to be out, either playing bridge or visiting friends. Rosa had sometimes wondered if mother and son ever met. One thing for sure, she showed no inclination to become involved in his troubles.

Rosa decided she would phone again the next morning as soon as she reached the office. It was important that she speak to Jeremy before Thursday.

"Get the Scott-Pearce Chelsea number for me please, Steph," she said, as she passed through their small reception area on Tuesday morning. It was shortly after nine o'clock and if the household was still asleep, it was time they were woken up.

She had only just reached her room along the passage when her phone gave a peremptory buzz.

307

"I have Mrs Scott-Pearce on the line," Stephanie announced and made the connection.

"Mrs Scott-Pearce speaking," said a colourless voice. "Who is that?"

"Rosa Epton. I don't believe we've spoken before, Mrs Scott-Pearce, but I'm your son's solicitor."

"He's mentioned your name."

"May I speak to him?"

"I'm afraid he's not here."

"When will he be back?"

"I don't think it'll be this week."

"Not this week?" Rosa echoed in a tone of dismay. "He's due to appear at Nettleford police station on Thursday to answer to his bail."

"I'm afraid I don't know anything about that . . . I seem to remember his saying he had to go back to Nettleford some time, but I don't think he mentioned a date. Perhaps you can explain to the police that he's away."

"Where's he gone?"

"He went to see his father. He left on Sunday. I believe they have a trip in mind."

"Did he say when he'd be back?"

"I don't think he knew how long he'd be away."

It was apparent to Rosa that Mrs Scott-Pearce knew very little about her son's movements and had scant interest in what he was up to.

"Did he not mention his appointment with the Nettleford police on Thursday?" she asked with a touch of exasperation.

"No. At least, I don't think so. He doesn't always keep me in touch with his activities."

"Do you know how I can get in touch with him?"

"You could phone his father's office in Geneva. They may be able to help you. Otherwise I'm afraid I can't suggest anything."

Rosa stifled her frustration. "Should Jeremy get in touch with you, Mrs Scott-Pearce, please ask him to call me as a matter of urgency. Remind him that he's due to present himself at Nettleford police station on Thursday."

"Yes, I'll certainly do that, Miss . . . er . . . . Epton," she said in the same tone she might have used if asked to remind him to pick up his laundry.

Rosa put through an immediate call to Charles Scott-Pearce's Geneva office only to be told he was travelling in Germany, but that he would be informed of Rosa's call when he phoned in. The person to whom Rosa spoke vouchsafed the belief that he was due to meet his son at some point on his travels.

It was not yet nine-thirty, but the day had begun badly. As far as Rosa could see, she was left holding the baby and had better decide on her best tactics vis-à-vis the police.

Tom phoned in mid-afternoon and said he had some important information which he wished to give her in person. He suggested he should drive up to town and take her out to dinner. Though Rosa secretly doubted the importance of the information, she was more than ready to be taken out to dinner.

He arrived at her flat shortly after seven-thirty and they set off immediately for her friendly Italian neighbourhood restaurant. Rosa often dropped in there when she couldn't be bothered to cook for herself and, like all their regular patrons, was always given a royal welcome.

"What's the important information?" she asked as they walked along the street.

"As I'd not heard anything from Mrs Palfrey about the gardening job, I phoned a couple of times this morning, but couldn't get a reply. So at lunchtime I decided to go to the house. Guess what?"

"There was nobody at home."

"More than that, the whole place was shut up. Blinds were pulled down and there wasn't a soul about."

"Because they've gone to Shrewsbury for Sir Clement Palfrey's funeral. He died last week and I found out this afternoon that he's being buried on Thursday." Tom gave a small pout of annoyance at being pre-empted. Rosa went on, "Sir Clement's death was announced in yesterday's *Times* and I called his home this afternoon to ask for details of the funeral."

★ ★ ★

"How do you know that's where Mrs Palfrey and family have gone?"

"Intelligent guesswork."

"Oh, is that all!"

"Don't sound so contemptuous."

"I'm sorry."

"I forgive you," she said, slipping her arm through his.

"But I'm not convinced you're right."

"About what?"

"Where Nadine Palfrey has skipped to."

"Where else should she have gone?"

"Somewhat further afield than Shrewsbury," he said in a thoughtful tone.

"What makes you say that, Tom?"

"I'm still sure that the answer to everything lies with her." He turned his head toward Rosa and said earnestly, "I think you ought to attend the funeral yourself."

"I can't. It's the day that Jeremy is due to report at Nettleford police station. Whether or not he'll turn up is another matter, but I must obviously be on hand."

"In that event, I'll go."

"All the way to Shrewsbury just to see who turns up at Sir Clement's funeral?" Rosa said in a startled voice. "Anyway, if Nadine Palfrey has really done a bunk, it's a matter for the police, if anyone. It's none of my business."

"It could affect your client's interests. I'll drive up overnight and count it as a day's sick leave."

"You're shameless."

"As a matter of fact I'm the most conscientious park-keeper on their books. I put in hours of overtime for which I'm never paid." He glanced about him. "How much farther is this restaurant? I'm thirsty and hungry and footsore."

"We're there," Rosa said, steering him through the door of Luigi's.

It was nearly eleven o'clock before they left and returned to Rosa's flat. She hadn't intended that he should stay the night, but somehow it worked out that way.

★ ★ ★

The next day Rosa tried a number of times to call Jeremy, but the phone always remained unanswered. Just before leaving the office to go home, she decided to ring Chief Inspector Harshaw. It seemed right to warn him of her client's likely failure to turn up. There was also an element of self-preservation in her decision. She didn't wish anyone to think that she had spirited him away.

"Detective Chief Inspector Harshaw speaking," he said with a daunting note of formality when the connection was made.

"It's Rosa Epton."

"Ah! I'm glad you've called, Miss Epton. What time will you and your client be coming tomorrow?"

"I fear I've been unable to get in touch with Jeremy Scott-Pearce. I spoke to his mother on Monday and she said he'd gone to visit his father and had not said when he'd be back. Since then I've phoned Mr Scott-Pearce's office in Geneva, but they were also unable to help."

"Are you trying to say that he's fled the country?"

"No; merely that I've been unable to get in touch with him. But that doesn't mean he won't appear tomorrow."

"Do you seriously believe that?"

"I don't know what to believe, but I thought it right to let you know the position."

"It's pretty clear to me that he's absconded. If he doesn't turn up, we'll get a warrant for his arrest."

"On what charge?"

"Murder, of course."

"Mr Palfrey's or Miss Seeberg's?"

"Mr Palfrey's in view of his admission of killing him. Other charges can, and almost certainly will, follow once we have him in custody. If he thinks he can play fast and loose with the process of law, he'll soon learn otherwise."

How soon was a matter for speculation, Rosa reflected. It had long been apparent that Jeremy was a thoroughly irresponsible young man, but that didn't make him a murderer.

"Do you now have evidence to justify charging him with Miss Seeberg's murder straightaway?"

"I'm not prepared to discuss the case on the phone," Harshaw said, leaving Rosa to wonder whether this was a further move in their game of bluff and deception. At all events there didn't seem much point in continuing their conversation.

"Unless I know for sure that my client will be answering to his bail tomorrow, I don't propose coming down. I can't believe he'll appear without first getting in touch with me, but should he turn up on your doorstep, I'd be grateful if you'd let me know immediately and not start interrogating him until I arrive."

"I'll see that you're informed of his arrival," Harshaw said, "but I'm not giving guarantees about anything else."

Rosa didn't altogether blame him for his attitude, though she wished he had been in a friendlier mood. She would like to have asked him if he knew about the Palfreys having apparently sealed their home and departed, but it was certainly not the time for importunate questions.

She had barely hung up when her telephone buzzed and Stephanie said, "I have a Mrs Fountain on the line. She wishes to speak to you."

"Fountain? Fountain? The name doesn't ring any bells with me. What does she want?"

"She's Miss Seeberg's sister."

"What on earth can she want?" Rosa echoed aloud. "OK, Steph, you'd better put her through."

"Am I speaking to Miss Rosa Epton?" a nervous voice enquired a moment later and went on, "My sister mentioned your name a number of times, so I hope it's all right to phone you — "

"Good afternoon, Mrs Fountain," Rosa broke in in an attempt to put her at her ease. "I didn't know your sister at all well, but I was very shocked to learn of her death."

"I kept on warning Madge, but she never listened. She was always inclined to be foolhardy and now look what's happened."

It seemed a quaint way of referring to a callous murder, though her meaning was clear.

"Warned her about what?" Rosa asked.

"Not to go nosing into Mr Palfrey's death. Let the police get on with it, I said every time we spoke, but I knew my words were falling on deaf ears. She just had to poke and pry. She was sure she knew who had killed Mr Palfrey." Mrs Fountain's voice was lowered to a whisper. "His name begins with 'C'. I obviously can't call the firm, not with Mr 'C' still there, so I decided to speak to you."

"Where are you phoning from?"

"From Nettleford. I'm at Madge's bungalow. I came down by train this morning. As Madge's next of kin, the police informed me of her death and I decided to come at once. I've always had a spare set of her keys in case of an emergency, just as she had mine."

"But why exactly are you calling me, Mrs Fountain?" Rosa asked, wondering if she had missed something.

"I want to search the bungalow, but I'd like to have somebody with me when I do so. Madge always spoke well of you, Miss Epton, and I wondered if you would come and help me. I would, of course, pay for your time."

"What are you expecting to find?" Rosa enquired in a puzzled tone.

"The last time I spoke to Madge she mentioned having found a letter which solved the mystery of Mr Palfrey's death. When I told her to take it to the police she said she first wanted to put her theory to the test."

"Did she tell you anything more about this letter?"

"No. She was very mysterious about it."

"And you believe it's hidden somewhere in the bungalow?"

"Yes. Madge was always fond of tucking things away in different places. Once when she had a large sum of money in the house for a few days — it was when she was going to buy a microwave oven in a sale — she sewed it into a cushion."

"Have you begun searching yet?"

"No. I'm nervous about doing it on my own. If we do find the letter, you'll know better than me what to do. So will you help me, Miss Epton?"

"I'll be glad to," Rosa said without further hesitation.

★ ★ ★

The next morning Rosa drove to Nettleford. She balked at the thought of telling the police where to find her in the event of Jeremy turning up at the station (though this seemed a more forlorn hope with each hour that passed without news of him) and instead gave Madge Seeberg's number to Stephanie with instructions to call her there if necessary. Stephanie's sense of judgment and discretion was faultless on such occasions.

She pulled up outside 16 Gillam Avenue shortly after ten-thirty. Mrs Fountain opened the front door before she had time to press the bell.

"I think somebody's tried to break in," she said in a fluttering voice as soon as Rosa was inside. "I didn't notice until I walked round the back this morning. There are marks on the frame of the bathroom window as if someone had tried to force it open."

"Did you hear any sounds in the night?"

Mrs Fountain gave a shudder. "No. I think it could have happened before I came, but I certainly shan't stop another night."

They were standing in the tiny hall and Rosa took the opportunity of sizing up Dolly Fountain. If Madge Seeberg had resembled a galleon under sail, her sister was more like a small tug, being short and plump with a head of straw-coloured clustered curls.

"Madge was always the intrepid one," she went on. "I used to warn her she'd come to a nasty end. But don't think I wasn't fond of her, because I was. Mind you, we'd never have got on if we'd lived together. Madge was too managing. That's why she never got married." As an afterthought she added, "Mr Fountain died four years ago." She paused and gave Rosa an anxious look. "I'm sorry, I don't usually talk as much as this. It must be nerves. Madge did most of the talking when we were together."

"Well, where shall we begin?" Rosa asked with a wry smile as she glanced about her.

* * *

Tom enjoyed his drive to Shrewsbury. He had always relished driving at night and was accustomed, when visiting his parents in Cumbria, to leaving home around midnight and arriving in time for a hearty breakfast.

On this occasion he stopped at a roadside café before going on into the city for an hour of mild sightseeing. The funeral was due to be held at eleven o'clock at a village church some five miles outside.

He arrived early and chose a seat at the back close to the door. By the time the service began and Sir Clement's coffin was carried in by four impassive pall bearers, he reckoned there were about fifty people present, presumably friends and neighbours. The notice in the *Times* had said 'funeral private' which, he supposed, meant that it wasn't an occasion for representatives of the various organisations with which Sir Clement had been associated during his life.

From his seat at the rear of the church, he was able to observe everything. Of Nadine Palfrey and her daughters, there was no sign at all.

He had previously attended only cremation services. Two; in each case for a friend who had been killed in a car accident. This was a much more solemn and drawn-out affair which concluded with the coffin being carried back down the aisle for interment in the churchyard outside. He remained in his place and watched the departing mourners, one or two of whom cast him curious glances.

Eventually the church was empty apart from himself and an elderly verger who was tidying up, pew by pew. As Tom approached him he paused in his labours and looked up.

"You from the press?" he enquired. Tom decided a nod was the simplest response and the verger went on, "Thought so. I can always tell. Also if you were a mourner, you'd be catching cold outside seeing the old boy being put under the sod."

Encouraged by the verger's apparent willingness to talk, Tom said, "I gather Sir Clement doesn't have any children, so who inherits the title?"

"He was never married, Sir Clement wasn't, and the baronetcy goes to some distant cousin. And that's a funny thing too, because the person who stood to inherit was recently killed in a shooting affair and the new baronet is still in his pram."

"Were any of that branch of the family at the service?"

The verger shook his head. "Mrs Palfrey, that's the baby's mother, phoned at the weekend and spoke to Mrs Hurst. She was Sir Clement's housekeeper; big, tall woman who was in the front pew, wearing a hat she might have borrowed from a scarecrow. Anyway, she told Mrs Hurst she was still recovering from her husband's sudden death and was being treated by the doctor for her nerves and she wouldn't be able to get to the funeral. She did send some flowers though. Mrs Hurst thought she should have made the effort to come, but as I said to her, I don't suppose Sir Clement will notice."

"Did you know Sir Clement well?"

He scratched his head in a ruminative way. "Must have known him about forty years. I used to do odd jobs up at the house. He was all right in his way," he added, not too enthusiastically.

Tom felt that he had learnt as much as he could and decided to leave the old man to continue his tidying up.

"It's been nice talking to you," he said, holding out his hand.

"My name's Wally Price if you want it for your article," the verger replied as he gave Tom's hand a warm shake.

As he returned to his car, Tom felt triumphant and totally vindicated. He must phone Rosa with the news as soon as he could find a call box.

★ ★ ★

Rosa sat staring at the letter while Mrs Fountain busied herself making coffee in the kitchen. They had found it (or rather Rosa had) tucked between the pages of a copy of *War and Peace*. There was a small bookcase in the sitting room, filled mostly with paperbacks which revealed Miss Seeberg's catholic taste. *War and Peace* and a dictionary were the only hardbacks.

There was an inscription in the Tolstoy novel which read:

To Madge Seeberg,
a loyal secretary,
with best wishes from Malcolm Palfrey,
Christmas 1984

It struck Rosa as an odd present to give one's secretary, even a loyal one, but maybe Miss Seeberg had specially requested it. Rosa didn't imagine that the title bore any significance.

She had turned the pages of the dictionary without finding anything more interesting than a recipe for Hungarian goulash which had fallen to the floor. Then, while Dolly Fountain investigated the drawers of a small corner cabinet, Rosa began her examination of *War and Peace*. The letter was lodged between pages four hundred and eighty-six and seven. The envelope was typewritten and addressed to: 'Amanda Ritchie, c/o Malcolm Palfrey, Palfrey and Co.' It had 'Please Forward' written in the top left-hand corner. It bore a London postmark and a date five days before Malcolm Palfrey's death. Inside was a single sheet of paper in a hand she immediately recognised. It read:

Dear Amanda,

I need to talk to you before the case and this seems to be the only way of getting in touch with you. Meet me at Pan's Place at nine pm. next Wednesday. I'll be there anyway. Please come.

Love, Jeremy.

As she read it, Rosa recalled Jeremy saying at their first meeting that he wanted to get in touch with Amanda, but didn't know where she was staying. It was natural enough to suppose that her solicitor would be aware of her address.

The letter had held no significance for Dolly Fountain, who had read it and gone off to the kitchen to make coffee.

To Rosa, however, it explained everything. Well, almost everything. It had clearly done the same for Madge Seeberg.

It was equally clear that Amanda Ritchie had never received the letter, it having been intercepted by Malcolm Palfrey, who had then kept the rendezvous at Pan's Place.

Moreover, he had gone there armed and prepared to kill, only to meet his own death. Rosa now felt that Jeremy's statement probably represented the basic truth of what happened, namely that Malcolm Palfrey had been shot with his own weapon in the course of a life and death struggle.

This had presumably also been Madge Seeberg's conclusion when she found the letter in a drawer of her employer's desk. The deduction that followed was less certain, but even more disturbing. It involved her confronting Jeremy with the truth and being murdered.

But what was the truth? If Jeremy had killed the solicitor in circumstances that plainly amounted to self-defence, he had little to fear, so what had Madge Seeberg discovered that caused him to add real murder to his list of crimes? There was only one answer and it was motive. What had been Malcolm Palfrey's motive for wishing to kill Jeremy?

Rosa felt that somehow she ought to know the answer. Indeed, that she did know it if only she could get her thinking cap on straight.

She was deep in thought when the telephone rang and Dolly Fountain came back into the room to answer it.

"It's for you," she said, holding out the receiver to Rosa.

"It's Stephanie," said a cool, dispassionate voice. "I've just had a call from Mr Berry. I told him you weren't available and he said to let you know that Mrs Palfrey and her daughters were not at the funeral. He'll phone you this evening."

"Thanks, Steph," Rosa said and rang off.

"Have you decided what to do with that letter?" Dolly Fountain enquired.

"I think the best course would be for you to take it to the police. You can tell them where it was found, but it might be better if you didn't mention my name. Say that you found it and are passing it on in case it's of any interest. Leave them to make what they can of it."

"All right, if that's what you advise." She paused. "Do you still think it was Mr Chance who murdered Madge?"

Rosa hesitated. "No. That's never been my belief."

"Who then?"

"I'm afraid it may have been a young man who is a client of mine and who has disappeared."

"But why? What motive could he have had?"

"That's what I'm still trying to figure out."

A few minutes later Rosa departed, after thanking Mrs Fountain and assuring her that there would be no charge for her professional services.

"Will it be all right to call you again if necessary?"

"Certainly, any time you wish."

Before heading back to London, Rosa decided to drive out to Kingsmere Farm and see if there were any signs of life. She took a slightly circuitous route as she didn't wish to be spotted in the town centre by anyone who knew her.

She found the house as Tom had described it, deserted and presenting a blank face on the surrounding garden and meadows.

So where had its occupants gone, if not to Sir Clement's funeral? And even more to the point, *why* had they left home so abruptly?

21

"I WISH we could go home," Cressida said gloomily.

"So do I," her sister replied.

They were sitting on the verandah of a villa overlooking the Adriatic north of Rimini.

"Mummy still hasn't said why we've come or why we had to leave in such a hurry."

"I believe she's had a breakdown as a result of Daddy's death and people suffering from breakdowns don't behave rationally." Teresa spoke with the air of one experienced in the vagaries of adult behaviour.

"It's funny it happened on the very day she heard about old Sir Clement's death," Cressida remarked. "I wonder if that had something to do with it?"

"I don't see how," her sister observed with a touch of scorn.

"She couldn't face all the extra strain so soon after Daddy's death." She paused.

"That old woman who helps out in the kitchen gives Crispin a curtsy every time she sees him. She must think he's an archduke or something." She paused again, then said in a thoughtful tone, "Are you glad we have a brother with a title?"

"I don't believe in titles," Teresa said in a superior tone. "In fact, I think they should be abolished."

"Are you also against the Queen?"

"Not in a personal sense, but in my view the monarchy has outlived its usefulness."

Cressida gave her sister a quizzical look. "Is that what your new history teacher says?"

"It's my own opinion," Teresa retorted crossly.

"I found a cockroach in my room last night," Cressida said, opening up a fresh topic of conversation.

"How revolting! What did you do?"

"Killed it with my bedroom slipper. It made a crunching sound."

"Oh, don't be so disgusting, you're making me feel sick."

At that moment, their mother appeared

at the other end of the verandah and came towards them.

"Isn't it a lovely view from here?" she remarked cheerfully.

"We'd both sooner be at home," Cressida replied firmly.

Nadine frowned. "I'm sure you'll get to like it here."

"But how long are we going to stay?" Teresa asked.

"I can't say, darling. It depends on several things."

"What things?"

"Don't ask so many questions, darling."

"But we want to know, Mummy," Cressida put in. "It's not knowing that's so unsettling. Is it all to do with Daddy's death?"

"In a way, yes."

"Are you worried that the police have got on to something?"

"I've given the police all the help I can."

"So what is it?"

"I thought we could all do with a break after the strain of recent weeks and since great aunt Emilia offered us the use of the villa, it seemed a good idea to come out here and recover our spirits. And now I must go and find out what Crispin and Maria are up to."

"She doesn't want to tell us, does she?" Cressida remarked.

"It makes me feel like a fugitive from justice," Teresa said in a dramatic tone.

Cressida was thoughtful for a time. "Do you know something," she said, breaking her silence, "I believe Mummy's afraid."

"Afraid of what?" Teresa asked with a frown.

"Afraid of reporters and all their questions. I'm sure our being here is linked to Sir Clement Palfrey's death."

"That's just your imagination. The truth is, Mummy's having a nervous breakdown and we must try and be patient with her. Perhaps the change of scene will do her good, even if it doesn't do anything for us."

Cressida knew it was a waste of time to argue when her older sister clambered on to one of her high horses. She decided to go to her room and write a letter to her best friend, Louise. She had not even had time to say goodbye to her before leaving.

Half-way along the bedroom corridor she came upon another cockroach and steered it into Teresa's room. It was always satisfying to have the last word in one of their arguments.

* * *

A couple of hundred miles north in a village in the mountains near Merano, Jeremy Scott-Pearce and his father sat in the bar of their hotel.

"The police won't trace you here for some time, even if they try," Charles Scott-Pearce remarked.

"They'll try all right," Jeremy observed grimly.

"Well, even if they put out a red alert or its equivalent, you won't be found in a hurry. That doesn't, however, solve the problem, it merely provides time."

They had been staying in the village for five days, going for long walks in the mountains and spending each evening in the bar. It was a perfect place to go to ground. Nobody spoke more than two words of English and the hotel, which had only eight bedrooms, was patronised by Italians who lived and worked on the Lombardian plain to the south or by Austrians who had come over the Brenner Pass to remind themselves that the district had once been part of their empire.

Many was the hour that father and son had spent discussing future plans without reaching any firm decision.

"I'd be picked up as soon as I arrived at Heathrow and then spend the rest of my life behind bars," Jeremy said.

"Now you're being dramatic," his father replied. "You don't know what evidence they have against you in respect of Madge Seeberg's death. It may be wafer thin. Indeed, they might not have any at all, provided you keep your trap shut."

"Interfering old bat," Jeremy said in a vicious tone.

Ignoring the comment, his father went on, "I think the best thing will be if I try and find out exactly what they do have against you. Miss Epton should be able to help. If not, I'll tap another source. I still have useful contacts in the area. At all events, I'll have to go back to Geneva at the weekend, I've already been away longer than I intended. But you'll be all right here for another week."

"If I don't die of boredom."

"There are worse fates than that," his father remarked brutally. "If tomorrow's a nice day, we'll have a final walk and fill our lungs with clean mountain air." He gave his son a sudden fond glance. "Cheer up and leave it to me to straighten things out.

"God, I've made a hash of my life," Jeremy exclaimed in an emotional outburst. "I've done nothing but cause trouble. I can't see how even you can get me out of this mess.

"Have another drink," his father said.

★ ★ ★

It was with enormous relief that Adrian Chance learned that there was a warrant out for Jeremy Scott-Pearce's arrest. Though it didn't mean that his troubles were at an end, at least the immediate pressure was off. He must keep his fingers crossed and hope that his peculation would never come to light. The fact was that he had used some £10,000 of a client's money; enough, at worst, to earn him a prison sentence and at least a summons to explain himself to the Law Society's disciplinary committee. But now the money had been put back and he could only pray that he had managed to do so without the original, illicit withdrawal becoming apparent.

He was sure that Malcolm Palfrey had become suspicious, even though his senior partner had never confronted him with his suspicions. And then Palfrey's sudden death, instead of lifting the pressure, had added to it, as sooner or later an audit of the firm's accounts seemed inevitable as part of the settling up of his estate.

And having Miss Seeberg around the office was a further cause of anxiety. They had never liked one another and he felt nervous every time he met her in a corridor, not knowing whether Palfrey had imparted his suspicions to his faithful secretary.

His visit to her bungalow on the evening she died had been intended to find out what, if anything, she knew. It was going to be a delicate mission, but one he felt driven to undertake. But it had been overtaken by events.

Fortunately the warrant for Jeremy's arrest and the strange disappearance of Nadine Palfrey and her children had taken the heat off him. The police were like a pack of blood-hounds which had, at last, picked up a scent. His hope was that it would lead them up hill and down dale for as long as possible. Meanwhile, he determined to maintain a low profile and trust that time would somehow render his defalcation less apparent, if not less culpable.

22

ROSA was now certain that Jeremy Scott-Pearce was a murderer. It was a thought that filled her with despair tinged with a sense of resignation. Looking back she could see an inexorable course of events.

She had defended a number of murderers in her career (that is to say, people charged and duly convicted of the crime), but this was the first time that somebody she was representing had resorted to murder after becoming her client. She found herself quietly inveighing against Malcolm Palfrey whom she regarded as the source of all their trouble.

It was he who had shunted his client on to her and it was his death that had precipitated everything that followed. Moreover, his death was entirely his own fault. He had gone out to commit murder and had ended up dead. It served him right, she reflected angrily. She felt indignant at having been catapulted into such a calamitous train of events. Admittedly Jeremy Scott-Pearce was no innocent, though, in one sense, he too had been sucked into the maelstrom. If she was correct in her reconstruction of events, Jeremy had shown great wickedness, but still not as much as Malcolm Palfrey, who had been motivated by vanity and greed. She recalled that Peter Chen had labelled him a charlatan the only time they met. Later she had revised her view of him to some extent, but Peter had been right.

When she returned to London after the discovery of the letter in Madge Seeberg's bungalow, all the pieces of the puzzle were in place save for one. Motive. Why had Malcolm Palfrey wanted to kill Jeremy? It must have been a desperate need for him to have run the appalling risk of discovery.

It was the next day that she had one of those blinding flashes of recollection that the subconscious releases from time to time. She remembered the first time she had spoken to Charles Scott-Pearce. He had phoned from Geneva not long after Jeremy had been to see her in the office. He had asked if Malcolm Palfrey had mentioned Jeremy's previous trouble and, when she professed ignorance, had gone on to tell her how he had been expelled from school for blackmailing a master who had subsequently committed suicide. It had sounded a particularly nasty matter, especially when one realised the perpetrator was a schoolboy.

Blackmail was a facet of character, a behavioural pattern rather than a one-off piece of conduct.

What if Jeremy had been blackmailing Malcolm Palfrey? One might have expected him, as a well-known solicitor in the community, to have gone straight to the police. But he had not done so and there could be only one explanation for that. He dare not.

For a while Rosa puzzled over this. Could it be that Jeremy had discovered that Palfrey had behaved unprofessionally in some matter where disclosure could spell ruin? It was possible, but didn't strike her as likely.

Then she fell to thinking about the solicitor's obsessive eagerness to have an heir, so that he could pass on the title he was due to inherit to his own son. Young Crispin had been born when his parents might reasonably have given up hope of any further children. Moreover, he had been born in Italy where Nadine was allegedly visiting family at the time. It showed, to say the least, a curious element of miscalculation on his parents' part.

Supposing, however, he was not Nadine's natural child, but had been adopted and brought back to England as her own baby? Rosa knew that adopted children were debarred from inheriting titles, so if it ever became known that Crispin was not their child, there would be the makings of a first-class scandal, of the sort that would provide the tabloid press with a field day.

She sat back and reviewed the scenario she had etched so far. Satisfied that it could be sustained, the next piece of supposition involved Jeremy's knowledge of what had happened. This, she felt, could be explained by his friendship with Nadine whom he regarded as a surrogate mother. Not hard to imagine that she had let slip something that had alerted him. She may even have told him their dark secret.

Blackmail of her husband followed.

And that's the point at which I came in, Rosa reflected wryly. Malcolm Palfrey obviously decided he no longer could, or wished to, defend Jeremy. Subsequent interception of Jeremy's letter to Amanda presented him with an opportunity he had probably been waiting for. Blackmail was always a risky trade.

Rosa got up from her desk and decided to try out her theory on Robin. She found him drafting a reply to a client who was noted for his irate and abusive letters.

"I've told him to look for another solicitor," Robin said. "He's written me one letter too many and we'll be well shot of him, even if he does help pay the rent. So now tell me something cheerful."

Sitting down in his visitor's chair, Rosa detailed her reconstruction of events at Nettleford. He listened without interruption until she had finished.

"I don't think I can pick any holes in that," he said. "It sounds most persuasive. I suppose he killed Miss Seeberg because she got on to the truth the same way as you did. He presumably found out that she was going to lay another floral tribute at Pan's Place that evening and waited for her."

"That's the one thing he can't be forgiven, murdering a harmless old secretary."

"The truth was that she wasn't harmless as far as he was concerned," Robin remarked. "And where do you suppose Mrs Palfrey has got to?"

"My guess would be Italy, where she has family. I suspect she couldn't face media interest in the new baronet and fled."

"Surely the press wouldn't show much interest in Sir Crispin?"

"Not the national press, I agree. But I bet the *Nettleford Gazette* would want to run a story about him. You know the sort of thing, Robin: 'Ancient title inherited by local toddler from eighty-six-year-old relative'. The mere prospect of that would have been sufficient to get Nadine Palfrey packing her bags. Assuming, that is, I'm right about Crispin not being her own child."

345

Robin gave a thoughtful nod. "Presumably adoption laws in Italy are laxer than here."

"I don't suppose for a moment this was a legal adoption. In a country where the church sets its face against both contraception and abortion, there must be quite a few unwanted babies born, either to young, unmarried girls or to some unfortunate woman who already has more children than she can care for. After all, the Palfreys were in a position to offer a good home."

"So Sir Crispin is probably a *bambino* from the slums of Naples."

"That's my guess."

"So, what are you going to do now?"

"What I've been doing most of the time, sitting tight and waiting on events. I certainly don't intend to offer my theory to the police."

"I agree you can't do that while Jeremy Scott-Pearce remains your client." Robin flung out his arms in a luxurious stretch. "Malcolm Palfrey should have stuck to being a lawyer," he remarked, "he was a total bungler when it came to murder."

★ ★ ★

Tom came to the flat that evening and Rosa made spaghetti bolognese, which she knew he liked.

Before they ate she told him of her theory of events, while he sat on the floor resting his head against her thigh.

"You really are a bright girl," he said in an admiring tone when she finished. "You've worked it all out."

"I feel I ought to have done so sooner."

"How could you? The final pieces only fell into place recently. Until Jeremy skipped out of the country and Nadine Palfrey upsticked and left home, it was still a continuing saga." He was thoughtful for a while, then he said, "What do you think Jeremy will do?"

"What would you do if you were in his place?" Rosa asked.

A full minute passed before he answered. "I've always believed that fate catches up with you sooner or later," he said in a reflective tone. "Therefore I'd probably come home and face the music. After all, the police may not have much of a case against him in respect of Miss

Seeberg's death and, provided he kept his big mouth shut, he could get off. In fact they may not even have enough to charge him. Anyway, with you defending him, he'd stand as good a chance as he could hope for." He turned his head and looked up into Rosa's face. "Why are you looking so mournful?"

"Was I? The truth is I don't particularly relish defending him further. I know that solicitors aren't obliged to love, admire or even respect their clients, but there's something about Jeremy Scott-Pearce that repels me. He's begun to haunt me like the smell of bad fish."

Tom gave her an amused glance. "If he doesn't come back, what's the alternative? I suppose he could wander about the world at his father's expense, traipsing from country to country. He might even be able to change his identity and settle somewhere. Make a fresh start and all that jazz. But he'd always be looking over his shoulder and if he shares my philosophy, he'd know it was merely a matter of time before fate caught up with him."

"Personally, I'd sooner he risked it."

"You mean you'd like him to go free

despite what he's done?"

"I'm his lawyer, not his creator and judge."

"You're evading the question."

"I know. What's more, I shall continue to evade it." She bent and kissed the top of his head. "And what about you, Tom? Surely you're not proposing to be a park-keeper for the rest of your life. You must have thoughts about the future."

"I shall stay at Shilman Green for another six months."

"And then?"

"If I haven't been able to persuade you to marry me, I shall go to Australia."

"Those are rather dramatic alternatives."

"I'm a dramatic sort of person," he replied.

23

THE next evening, Friday, Rosa took home a pile of work to occupy her over the weekend, which she was planning to spend on her own.

On Saturday morning, however, she received an unexpected invitation to attend a Mahler concert at the Festival Hall that night. Paul Maxted, a barrister, whom she frequently briefed, called to say he had a spare ticket and would she go with him? It seemed that one of their children had been taken ill during the night and his wife felt she must stay at home and look after him.

"He'll probably be all right again by this evening, but she'd only worry if she came, so will you accompany me, Rosa?"

Rosa accepted with pleasure and in the event enjoyed both the concert and Paul's company. As she sat in enraptured silence listening to Mahler's fourth symphony she reflected once more that music was a magical therapy for the tired and harassed spirit.

The effect was still with her the next day as she worked her way through the papers in her briefcase.

On Monday morning the spell was broken by a couple of lines in the 'News in Brief' column of her paper. It read:

Jeremy Scott-Pearce, aged 22 of London, died in a fall near Merano in the Italian Alps on Saturday.

For a moment she felt like a drowning person whose life is said to pass before their eyes during their final seconds.

As soon as she reached the office she tried to call Mrs Scott-Pearce at her flat in Chelsea but, as so often, there was no reply. She then put through a call to Geneva to be informed that Mr Scott-Pearce had had to leave suddenly and it wasn't known when he would be back.

Rosa despatched Ben, their young outdoor clerk, to buy all the papers he could find. These, however, provided her with no additional information. Only two of them carried the news and one didn't mention Jeremy's name.

The effect of Mahler having now completely worn off, Rosa could only wait with impatience for the first edition of an evening paper. This, at least, contained more details.

She read that he had been staying alone following his father's departure. The proprietor of the hotel said that 'the young Englishman' had seemed depressed and had spent more and more time drinking in the bar. On Saturday afternoon he had gone out for a walk and not returned. It was thought he had either slipped or been carried over the edge of a ravine by a fall of snow. A goat-herd had observed him from a distance. One moment he was on the narrow track, the next he had disappeared. There was a strong wind at the time with a lot of snow being blown about. By the time a rescue team found him, he was dead.

Tuesday's newspapers all carried an account of sorts, but only one gave any further information. The Daily Post reported that Mr Charles Scott-Pearce, 'a wealthy businessman who lives in Geneva', had arrived in the village where it had happened and had expressed the wish that his son's body should be buried locally.

When Rosa called Detective Chief Inspector Harshaw he said that he had, indeed, read the reports and was seeking further information through Interpol. He seemed to regard it as a personal slight that Jeremy's body was not being brought back for burial in England.

"I suppose you'd heard about Mrs Palfrey, Miss Epton?"

"I knew she'd gone away."

"Not only gone away, but staying away. She's proposing to live in Italy and has put Kingsmere Farm up for sale. It's understandable that it has unhappy memories for her. It seems she doesn't wish her small son to inherit the baronetcy and is doing whatever's necessary to renounce the title. Seems a funny thing to do, but that's her business." He let out a sigh. "An unsatisfactory ending to a most unsatisfactory enquiry," he said in an almost accusing tone. "I'm referring to young Scott-Pearce's demise. Now I can't question him about why he rented a car the evening Miss Seeberg was killed and left his own parked outside his mother's flat. Did you know that, Miss Epton?"

Rosa hadn't known and decided to remain silent.

And there the matter rested until, about ten days later, she received a letter postmarked Geneva. As she opened the envelope a cheque for two thousand five hundred pounds fluttered to the floor and lay face upwards. She let it stay there until she had read the letter.

Dear Miss Epton,

As you will doubtless have read, Jeremy died in an accident in the Italian Alps and now lies buried in that country. A funeral at home would have stirred up too much curiosity and speculation, which would not have benefited anyone. We were together until the day before his death when I left to return to Geneva.

354

I can't say what the future might have held, had he lived. He was my son and we were very fond of one another. I feel badly about having failed him at various times in his short life, but I'm not the only parent to suffer that sort of remorse.

The proprietor of the hotel where he was staying told me that he hit the bottle hard after I left. He was concerned when Jeremy ventured forth on his own that afternoon in treacherous conditions.

Jeremy's statement about Malcolm Palfrey's death was the truth. I have no pity for Malcolm who tried to murder my son, whatever his motive. He was a pompous old cheat and even if blackmail can never be justified, there are occasions when one need not feel sorry for the victim. But enough said about that. Miss Seeberg's death was a direct consequence of everything that had gone before. I'm sure Jeremy deeply regretted it, but he felt his security was threatened and didn't have sufficient maturity to deal with the situation.

"Yuk!" Rosa murmured in a contemptuous aside, as she prepared to read on.

I'm sorry I wasted your time with my false statement. Jeremy and I cooked the idea up together when he came out here on a flying visit. We felt the police were fair game for a bit of confusion. Jeremy called you from Heathrow when he got back and was himself confused when you queried where he was phoning from, because you could hear background noise.

I am proposing to send the police at Nettleford a short, edited version of events which will enable them to close their file. They will doubtless still be after my blood, but I shan't be coming to England for several months and will decide how to handle that situation when it arises. That apart I shall be glad if you will clear up the mess. The further cheque is to that end. Let me know if it's not sufficient.

Thank you for all your help, both to myself but more particularly to Jeremy.

Yours sincerely,

Charles Scott-Pearce.

PS Jeremy used to say he wished he had a girlfriend like you. I hope that doesn't offend.

Rosa bent down and slowly picked the cheque up from the floor.

I'm not offended, she thought, but I'm not flattered either. I just hope that Nettleford remains off my map for the rest of time.

Later it occurred to her that Chief Inspector Harshaw might regard Jeremy's death as an unsatisfactory end to the case, but it had certainly resolved her own dilemma — or one of them.

Other titles in the
Ulverscroft Large Print Series:

TO FIGHT THE WILD
Rod Ansell and Rachel Percy

Lost in uncharted Australian bush, Rod Ansell survived by hunting and trapping wild animals, improvising shelter and using all the bushman's skills he knew.

COROMANDEL
Pat Barr

India in the 1830s is a hot, uncomfortable place, where the East India Company still rules. Amelia and her new husband find themselves caught up in the animosities which seethe between the old order and the new.

THE SMALL PARTY
Lillian Beckwith

A frightening journey to safety begins for Ruth and her small party as their island is caught up in the dangers of armed insurrection.

THE WILDERNESS WALK
Sheila Bishop

Stifling unpleasant memories of a misbegotten romance in Cleave with Lord Francis Aubrey, Lavinia goes on holiday there with her sister. The two women are thrust into a romantic intrigue involving none other than Lord Francis.

THE RELUCTANT GUEST
Rosalind Brett

Ann Calvert went to spend a month on a South African farm with Theo Borland and his sister. They both proved to be different from her first idea of them, and there was Storr Peterson — the most disturbing man she had ever met.

ONE ENCHANTED SUMMER
Anne Tedlock Brooks

A tale of mystery and romance and a girl who found both during one enchanted summer.

CLOUD OVER MALVERTON
Nancy Buckingham

Dulcie soon realises that something is seriously wrong at Malverton, and when violence strikes she is horrified to find herself under suspicion of murder.

AFTER THOUGHTS
Max Bygraves

The Cockney entertainer tells stories of his East End childhood, of his RAF days, and his post-war showbusiness successes and friendships with fellow comedians.

MOONLIGHT
AND MARCH ROSES
D. Y. Cameron

Lynn's search to trace a missing girl takes her to Spain, where she meets Clive Hendon. While untangling the situation, she untangles her emotions and decides on her own future.

NURSE ALICE IN LOVE
Theresa Charles

Accepting the post of nurse to little Fernie Sherrod, Alice Everton could not guess at the romance, suspense and danger which lay ahead at the Sherrod's isolated estate.

POIROT INVESTIGATES
Agatha Christie

Two things bind these eleven stories together — the brilliance and uncanny skill of the diminutive Belgian detective, and the stupidity of his Watson-like partner, Captain Hastings.

LET LOOSE THE TIGERS
Josephine Cox

Queenie promised to find the long-lost son of the frail, elderly murderess, Hannah Jason. But her enquiries threatened to unlock the cage where crucial secrets had long been held captive.

THE TWILIGHT MAN
Frank Gruber

Jim Rand lives alone in the California desert awaiting death. Into his hermit existence comes a teenage girl who blows both his past and his brief future wide open.

DOG IN THE DARK
Gerald Hammond

Jim Cunningham breeds and trains gun dogs, and his antagonism towards the devotees of show spaniels earns him many enemies. So when one of them is found murdered, the police are on his doorstep within hours.

THE RED KNIGHT
Geoffrey Moxon

When he finds himself a pawn on the chessboard of international espionage with his family in constant danger, Guy Trent becomes embroiled in moves and countermoves which may mean life or death for Western scientists.